"I have a plan to disrupt electrical power across America," Lydia said. "Deprived of power, the humans would be at a distinct disadvantage. Their computers, their manufacturing facilities, much of their communications systems—none of it would work without electricity."

"But much of their communications equipment can be run by generators or batteries."

"Not if we detonate a small number of nuclear warheads high overhead. It'll cause an electromagnetic pulse that will disrupt all communications without exception. Then we can invade the continent under cover of night and chaos. Fallout will be minimal."

When she was gone, Barry allowed himself to feel stunned for the first time. Somehow, he had to contact Donovan . . .

Other V books from Pinnacle

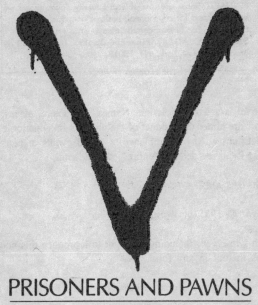

PRISONERS AND PAWNS

Howard Weinstein

PINNACLE BOOKS **NEW YORK**

V: PRISONERS AND PAWNS

Copyright © 1985 by Warner Bros., Inc.

An original Pinnacle Books edition, published for the first time
anywhere.

First printing/March 1985

ISBN: 0-523-42439-6

Can. ISBN: 0-523-43420-0

Printed in the United States of America

PINNACLE BOOKS, INC.
1430 Broadway
New York, New York 10018

9   8   7   6   5   4   3   2   1

Author's Notes

Not long after Ann Crispin and I finished working on *V: East Coast Crisis*, I was asked to tackle another *V* novel as part of a series of five original books based on the TV mini-series and the just-announced weekly series due to start the following autumn. (This was back in May 1984, just after the second *V* mini-series garnered smash-hit ratings for NBC.)

These books were targeted to hit the stands during *V*'s first season on television, which meant that they had to be written very quickly, before the series had even started production on weekly one-hour episodes. It also meant the writers of the first two or three novels would be working in something of a vacuum—the format for the weekly *V* series was only then being shaped by a staff of frantic writers and producers out in California. Early scripts and a "TV Writers Guide" might not be ready in time to do those intrepid novelists any good at all.

I said a silent prayer for my fellow book writers and opted to do the fourth novel, which would give me more time to match my story to what you will have been seeing on television since *V* debuted in October. At this writing, that event hasn't yet taken place (it's early September now), and I can only hope that the TV series has been good enough—and popular enough—that it's still on the air as you pick up this novel.

As many of you know, it's not uncommon for a new television series to have a life expectancy similar to that of a person floating in the void of space—without benefit of a spacesuit.

What will *V*'s fate be? Who knows?

If the writers, producers, actors, and all the other talented people who work on a TV series have the time to craft this show the right way, it could have a long run. Decent action-adventure, with a little thoughtful substance mixed in, could make for pretty good television.

V: PRISONERS AND PAWNS was written after I'd read the first few stories intended for the television series, so I've followed the series continuity, using the characters you've seen on TV. But it was written before I'd *seen* any of the new weekly episodes, so it's my own interpretation of how the series might be done.

I hope you enjoy it!

Howard Weinstein
September 1984

PRISONERS
AND
PAWNS

Chapter 1

The full moon shone down on the California desert, bathing the parched land in ghostly pale light. A coyote padded along softly, carefully, ears set as he listened for the movement of potential meals among the scrubby weeds and brush. He stopped, licked the fur of one front paw, then coughed out a short howl.

A movement overhead caught his eye, and his nostrils twitched as he tried to catch a scent.

But the Visitor skyfighter gave off only the faint whispering *whoosh* of its antigrav drive. The coyote yawned and resumed his search.

The small alien spacecraft flew by on a search of its own. Its duckbilled nose cone reflected the moonlight. Inside, two Visitor pilots sat in the cockpit while a third officer manned the gun turret in the aft compartment. All wore red coverall uniforms with black stripes of rank.

"Still no locator signal, sir," said Lawrence, the younger officer up front, running a hand through his black hair. He had a thin, pleasant human face. But underneath his artificial skin, he was a dark, scaly-skinned reptile. He glanced at his mission commander, Captain Simon. Simon's human skin had been damaged in a terrorist attack the previous day, and he hadn't yet had time for cosmetic repairs. He'd simply peeled it off his upper body, giving him a strange hybrid appearance—human hands and arms but with his normal glistening scales visible on his torso and face.

1

Seeing Simon without his humanlike casing made the younger officer long for home. It had been many months since the Visitors received Diana's signal and reinvaded Earth upon discovery that the red-dust biological toxin the humans had developed against them worked only sporadically, depending partly on climate and other factors.

In his youthful exuberance, Lawrence had expected the reinvasion to proceed quickly. Without the toxin, how could these primitive humans fight the superior technology of the Visitors? But, as during the first occupation of the planet, humans proved they could fight against the odds. And now Lawrence found himself wondering from time to time, *We've taken so many losses, maybe we should give up and return to the home world. Maybe we can't win.*

"If this rendezvous isn't carried out as planned," Simon said, "Lydia's position as security chief could be in serious jeopardy. We could all move up in rank."

"Or we could all be court-martialed and executed, Simon."

The alien commander flicked his tongue across his lipless mouth. "Your optimism is showing again, Lawrence."

"With good reason. We both know how much Lydia and Diana hate each other. We both know that, given half a reason, one would willingly get rid of the other, along with all her allies. We, unfortunately, are rather strongly identified with Lydia."

"Not so unfortunate," Simon snapped, his voice throbbing as it rose defensively. "We're part of an elite force. Fleet Security gets special privileges others just dream about—or have you been spoiled by all that privilege?"

The younger officer hunched his shoulders. "I've never even met Diana, but some officers who have swear she's on the edge of insanity. She's turned on her own officers before—they say she even murdered Supreme Commanders John and Pamela during the first occupation."

"Murdering superior officers doesn't mean someone's insane. Not that *you* should get any ideas, Lawrence," Simon said warningly. "But that's how the Great Leader got to where he is. You know that's part of life in the fleet."

"I'd prefer it if that weren't part of *my* life in the fleet—especially if I get caught in some crazy power play between Diana and Lydia."

"Don't worry. Diana may be insane, but I don't think Lydia is. She won't start something unless she can finish it and come out on top," the captain said.

Lawrence shook his head, his hair falling across his brow. "She may not have a choice if these prisoners don't get delivered to Diana as ordered."

"You worry too much."

Lawrence glanced at the chronometer on the console. "I have reason to. Lydia was supposed to give us the signal three minutes ago."

Lawrence was about to continue when a red light winked insistently and an accompanying chime sounded.

"Like I said, you worry too much," Simon repeated. "Now, triangulate on that and calculate landing coordinates."

"Yes, sir," the younger alien answered, his fingers punching up a geographic grid on the computer screen.

Ham Tyler's finger pointed at the radar screen glowing green in the rear compartment of the four-wheel-drive Chevy Blazer.

"They've stopped circling," Tyler said. "I think they've found what they're looking for." He turned his wiry body slightly to face Mike Donovan, the TV news cameraman-turned-resistance-leader.

"You could be wrong," Donovan said with a little more belligerence in his voice than he'd intended. He and Tyler had a knack for bringing out the worst in each other. It wasn't something Donovan liked, since they had to work closely as key members of the California-based band of resistance fighters. But their antagonism was a fact of life, and Donovan couldn't bring himself to back down in their continual game of push and shove. "You've been wrong before."

"Not in *your* lifetime," Tyler answered evenly, leveling a cold gaze at Donovan. "Keep watching."

They both followed the blip on the screen. What had appeared as a random search pattern seemed now to be a purposeful flight. Though he hated to do it, Donovan had to admit that the ex-CIA agent knew what he was talking about—*this time*. "Okay," Donovan said. He reached for the radio mike.

"On scramble," Tyler said.

Donovan glared at him. "I know, Tyler. Back off. I've been fighting the Visitors as long as you have."

"Sure, but I've been fighting, *period*, since you were a choirboy. I've gotten us equipment you've never even seen before, and I just want to make sure you use it right."

Donovan considered a retort but held it in. "Prowler to Duster—come in, please," he said into the microphone.

At an airstrip ten miles away, a radio crackled to life in the small shed that served as the tiny airport's office. Julie Parrish brushed a strand of blond hair off her face and picked up the headset. "Prowler, this is Duster. Target located?"

"Located. Once you're airborne, we'll guide you," Donovan said. "Be careful, Julie. Good luck."

"We'll be fine," Julie said. "See you at the rendezvous."

She turned off the transmit switch, then faced the rest of her mission team.

"Why so serious, little girl?" asked Chris Faber, Ham Tyler's beefy friend and fellow ex-CIA operative.

Julie managed a semismile—Chris always called her "little girl." Coming from someone else, she might have resented it. But she knew he meant it with brotherly affection—he was a gentle-voiced, affable southerner who seemed unafraid of being courtly and thoughtful. He rarely followed the macho posturing of his friend Tyler, but Julie had to remind herself that Chris was just as capable of killing as Tyler, and Chris could do it as dispassionately as turning off a light switch. Chris ducked his head slightly to gaze into her eyes.

"Sorry," she said. "It's just that I don't like having to

rely so much on information slipped to us by Visitor fifth columnists.''

Chris shrugged. "I know what you mean. But in this business, you take info anywhere and any way you can get it—and then you take it with a grain of salt."

"You shouldn't worry, Julie," Willie said, his guileless face radiating its usual warmth and concern.

Julie smiled at him. It was easy to forget that Willie was a Visitor himself. It had been well over a year since he'd stayed behind on Earth after the first occupation had ended, and Julie had become certain that even if Willie stopped wearing his homely human face, they would still love him, lizard or not.

"Barry is a reliable fifth columnist," Willie continued reassuringly. "He gets information right from the—um— the horse's south."

Chris and Julie tried not to laugh at this latest of the alien's malapropisms. "That's horse's *mouth*, Willie," Julie corrected gently.

Willie's own mouth drooped in disappointment. "So long I am on your planet and I still can't speak your language."

Julie gave him a quick hug. "You're doing fine, Willie. Sometimes I like your way of saying things better anyway."

He flashed a lopsided smile. "You and Chris better go now. The ground forces will need your air cover."

"*If* Barry's Visitor information is right," Julie said, worry creeping back into her voice.

Willie raised his hand—with his thumb pointed down. Chris reached out, turned the alien's thumb up and matched the sign of optimism with one of his own.

"As soon as we're gone, Willie, you get your lizard hide outa here," Chris said. "You did your job. If anything goes wrong, we want you back at Club Creole, safe and sound."

Willie followed them out of the shed. The only light on the airstrip came from the blue-white moon. "I wish I could go with you," Willie said plaintively.

"I wish you could too, but this isn't exactly an airliner we're flying," Julie said, gesturing toward the small crop-duster biplane waiting on the runway. "There's only room for two."

Willie stood by and watched them climb into the old plane, Chris up front in the pilot's seat, Julie behind. When she was strapped in, wearing goggles and helmet, she lifted a shoulder-mounted missile launcher from the floor well and tested its feel and balance. "I sure hope I can shoot this thing straight," she said.

Chris glanced back. "Piece of cake, honey. If you're anywhere near the target, these heat-seeking shells'll do all the work. Besides, you've been able to handle every weapon you've picked up. You'll do fine."

"Thanks, Chris. Some people go bowling at night—we shoot down Visitor skyfighters."

"You got it, ace," Chris laughed. Then he started the plane's engine. It rolled ahead and taxied down the bumpy runway.

Willie watched as the biplane picked up speed, bounced down the strip, and finally lifted into the sky, rising sluggishly toward the moon. He whispered a prayer in his own language, then climbed into a four-wheel-drive wagon and drove away from the small airport, headed back to Los Angeles.

Donovan and Tyler lay on their bellies in the sand, peering over a ridge into the desert valley below. About a dozen resistance fighters in camouflage outfits stood or crouched behind them. Some carried semi-automatic firearms, while others had captured Visitor laser weapons. They were as heavily armed as a small troop of foot soldiers could be, but at the moment their leaders were engaged in an argument and they were going nowhere.

"I don't care what the scanners say," Donovan said. "You and I are looking at the same piece of real estate and neither of us is seeing Lydia and her prisoners."

"They're there, Gooder. We picked up their locator beacon, so they gotta be there," Tyler countered.

"Fine, but *where*?" Donovan snarled, tossing the binoculars back to Tyler.

* * *

Lydia checked the chronometer on the vehicle's instrument panel. She sat alone at the controls in the windowless cockpit, glancing at the sensor's visual analogue screens that told her what was going on outside. So far, no problems. One scanner indicated that Captain Simon's escort skyfighter was closing on their location. All was going according to plan, and Lydia allowed herself a satisfied half smile—she would get great pleasure out of completing this important mission for Diana, since she knew that Diana was poised anxiously, waiting for Lydia to make a major mistake.

After Diana had escaped from the humans and returned to her Mother Ship, she'd declared herself Supreme Fleet Commander, stepping into a power vacuum left by her having murdered the only officers who'd outranked her. Ever since, life had been . . . interesting, to say the least. As Fleet Security Chief, Lydia possessed genuine power, second only to Diana's. To maintain their respective positions, each needed the other's tacit cooperation. But it had been made quite clear that should either falter enough to jeopardize her power, the other would have no qualms about giving the push needed to cause the final, irrevocable fall. Thus, since Diana was her nominal superior, Lydia had to be at her sharpest at all times.

In some ways, Lydia thought with a sigh, her position was a thankless one, with no letup in pressure. On the one hand, her job as security chief was of vital importance to the success of the reinvasion of Earth, and Diana gave her assignments of the most critical nature. But every time Lydia completed another difficult task, it not only solidified her own position, it also made Diana look like an effective and daring field commander.

But if Lydia failed, the failure would be her own. Therefore, she had decided she simply would not—could not—fail. *Ever.* Sooner or later, Diana would make a mistake that couldn't be pinned on her subordinates—oh, the supreme commander was very good at *that*—and Lydia would be in position to take advantage and take over.

"Commander," a male Visitor voice said from the intercom speaker, *"is it time to surface yet?"*

"Yes, James. It's time. I'm coming back to see the prisoners."

She swung out of the control seat and stood to her full height. She was tall, slim, and light in complexion and hair—sharp contrast to the dark good looks of her rival, Diana. At first Lydia had found these human appearances disconcerting, even having a couple of nightmares where she thought she was actually transformed into a human being, but she'd finally made the adjustment. Still, it had been a long time since she'd looked like herself, she thought wearily.

The bulkhead hatchway slid open and Lydia stepped into the rear compartment of the vehicle. She leaned casually on the wall and looked at the trio of human prisoners sitting quietly inside their power-field cubicles.

On her left was David Durning, the balding American. He was in his forties and completely nondescript looking. She'd never have guessed him to be a top secret agent. But that, perhaps, was what made him so effective at his work.

In the center was Susan Coopersmith, a spectacularly lovely British spy. Diana might enjoy this human in more ways than one, Lydia thought distastefully. Diana's insatiable appetite for sex with humans of both genders made Lydia blanch. Torturing and eating a freshly killed human being was acceptable, but sexual contact with these creatures was something Lydia couldn't stomach. *Oh, well, perhaps it'll be Diana's downfall someday.*

And, finally, the Japanese man, Kyoshi Maragato. Compact, bald headed, unemotional, and a deadly practitioner of hand-to-hand martial arts, as Lydia's security troops had discovered when they kidnapped Maragato in Tokyo. He'd killed two hulking Visitor agents before four more subdued him.

Capturing these three—three of the most important human intelligence agents on the planet—hadn't been easy. There had been many trails to follow, many informants to pursue. At last the pieces had fallen together, though the whole project wouldn't have been possible without the cooperation of human collaborators—*traitors*. What counted was final results, especially since the capture of selected key agents had been Lydia's idea in the first place. Diana had balked at the amount of energy and resources that would be required, but Lydia had convinced her that these specially trained intelligence operatives were the main liaison between governmental authorities and the underground. Where governments had been forced to cease their open resistance to the Visitors, they'd often managed to maintain channels of aid and armaments to small rebel groups. Capturing those secret agents would not only disrupt the channels, it would also enable the Visitors to tap the information they carried in their brains.

"Very soon," Lydia said smoothly, "you'll be transferred to the Mother Ship and placed in Diana's custody. You know things that will be of great interest to us. You'll be questioned—"

"You mean tortured," Susan Coopersmith said in an icy voice.

Lydia smiled tolerantly. "You *will* reveal that information one way or another. Whether you reveal it easily and cooperatively—or painfully—is up to you." She looked at her junior officer, James, a boyish lieutenant with features that were at the same time darkly handsome and malevolent. "Engage engines, James."

He nodded. "Yes, Commander." He reached for a set of toggle switches on the wall and a powerful throbbing shook the vehicle to life.

With a disdainful last look at her prisoners, Lydia returned to the cockpit. What a crisply executed mission this would be. The humans had been brought here as planned, gathered together with a minimum of personnel because Lydia had to make up for the large number of Visitor agents initially needed to locate and capture the targets. Soon the humans would be transferred to the Mother Ship. Lydia's coup would be then completed— neatly, quietly, without attracting the attention of the local L.A.-area resistance.

V

* * *

Donovan peered at the luminous numbers on his watch. He and Ham were still side by side on the edge of the desert ridge. Their impatient troops sat on the ground.

"They're not out there," Donovan said flatly.

Tyler continued looking through the binoculars. "They're out there, Gooder."

"You are so goddamned stubborn. Why can't you just admit we were suckered, or Barry got the wrong information. Or maybe this whole thing was a decoy. I don't know—but I *do* know we're wasting our time. And even if they are here, I still don't see how a crop duster is going to take on a skyfighter."

"The skyfighters are too fast to fight with something as slow as a biplane. I wouldn't want to try to outrun one, but those Visitor rocket sleds just can't maneuver well at under four hundred miles an hour."

"What makes you so sure?"

"I supervised some of the tests myself after the war ended. Trust me, Donovan."

"As far as I can throw you." Donovan raised the binoculars again. "I'm telling you, they're not out there."

Tyler leaned on his elbow. "They are—I'll bet on it."

"Great," Donovan said sarcastically. "Let's bet. Where the hell are they—under the sand?"

Donovan turned his back in frustration. Tyler took the binoculars from him and gazed out over the rugged terrain.

"Yep, Gooder. They're under the sand," Tyler said in a smooth voice.

"Oh, right, under the sand." Donovan snickered, then reconsidered and decided maybe Ham wasn't kidding. In a quick motion, he rolled over, yanked the field glasses out of Tyler's hands—and found he didn't need them. About a quarter of a mile away, illuminated by moonlight, something was breaking through the desert surface like an impossible beast rising from the core of the planet.

He used the binoculars and saw it was no beast. It was a machine with some sort of swiveling boring device on its nose which was still spinning as it cut through the dirt and rock, allowing the vehicle to surface from its hiding place. The body was about the size of a small panel truck and it rode on tanklike treads. It had no visible armaments on its outside, but Donovan figured it must have ports of some kind that allowed weapons to be fired from the interior.

"We've breached the surface, Commander," said James, who'd moved to the cockpit and sat next to Lydia. He steered the vehicle while she fine-tuned the locator beacon to signal the approaching skyfighter.

"Beam locked on," Lydia said.

"Son of a bitch," Donovan whispered as he watched. "Good thing we didn't make the bet."

"We *did*," Ham said firmly. "We just didn't decide what it would be. We'll decide later," he finished before Donovan could protest.

Back in one of the four-wheel drives, a young man with a blond military haircut looked up from the scanning screens. "Ham, Mike, I've got two blips—the skyfighter is closing fast."

"What about Julie and Chris?" Donovan asked quietly, watching the night skies in search of both aircraft.

"They're circling, tightening the noose," said the young man, whose name was Dan.

"Radio exact coordinates, Danny boy," Tyler said. "Tell 'em it's time to make our move."

Dan did as he was ordered. Donovan took a deep breath. "This better work," he said.

Tyler looked at him for a moment, then nodded. "My buddy's up there too, Gooder. It'll work."

They heard the whispered approach of the skyfighter, then saw it banking in from the west. They also heard the chugging whine of the biplane's prop motor from the south. Then they saw it. Donovan felt a tightening in his stomach, but there wasn't much he could do about what was going to happen in the air. He decided he'd better occupy himself with the ground activities, and he turned to the waiting assault squad.

"Everybody ready?" He looked at their faces, acknowledged the nods of the dozen men and women, and licked his lips. "Okay, then, into formation, on alert."

Tyler stood back a bit, letting Donovan give the order. He knew that Donovan's rapport with the fighters was better than his. Sure, he knew these people had been businessmen and teachers and storekeepers and surf bums two years ago, and he knew they weren't long-time battle veterans, but he just didn't have the patience to coddle them. If that's what they needed now and then to get them to risk their necks like real men, then he'd let Donovan handle the public relations. When they were ready to mobilize, he'd step back in as co-commander.

The modified control panel of the old crop duster contained several special electronic extras, and Chris's trained eye ran quickly along them. A flashing green light winked at him. "We're in firing range, Julie," he murmured into his headset.

Julie hefted the launcher, bracing it in the cradle they'd installed on the plane's body. She loaded three small shells into the tubular firing chamber—all it could hold at one swallow.

"All set," she said.

"Duster to Prowler," Chris said. "Do you read?"

"We read," came the answer in Tyler's voice. "Danny boy will tell you when you're at optimum range."

Aboard the skyfighter, Lieutenant Lawrence leaned forward in his seat. "Captain," he said, staring at the sensor screens.

"What is it?"

"Another aircraft in the vicinity."

"One of ours?" Simon asked.

"No, sir. By configuration and air speed, it's a very old human airplane."

"What's it doing?"

"Just flying, Captain. It's not making any moves to intercept us or interfere."

Their radio transceiver chimed—a signal from Lydia's sand rover. "Captain, I've been monitoring your sensor readings—shoot that plane down. I want no chances taken with this mission—*none at all*. Is that clear?"

Lawrence and Simon exchanged glances. "Perfectly clear," Simon answered. "We're diverting now to intercept."

Dan's eyes stared unwaveringly at his readout screens in the Blazer's back seat. Tyler and Donovan stood just outside the small truck.

"That's it," Dan said. "The skyfighter's just veered off—heading right for Duster." The young resistance fighter adjusted the mouthpiece of his headset. "Julie, Chris—do you read? They're heading your way."

"We read you, Prowler. We'll take it from here," said Julie. "You do your part down there. See you on the ground when we're all done."

"Are you sure this is going to work?" Julie said to Chris.

"Theoretically," he answered over the engine's droning.

"That's *not* what I wanted to hear." On her night scope, she could see the skyfighter quickly approaching. "What do you mean?"

"If we do it right, no way do we lose."

"That's more like it," Julie said.

Chris banked the little plane hard over to their left and turned to face the skyfighter head-on. Julie couldn't see it from her rear seat, but Chris's mouth spread into a wide grin.

Simon stared at the main viewscreen and its computer-enhanced night image, an image of a tiny air vehicle bearing on what seemed to be a collision course. "Are these humans insane?"

"I don't know," Lawrence said, answering the rhetorical question. "Maybe they don't see us with our running lights off."

In the aft compartment, the gunner intently watched her

own screen, with its forward view showing the odd little aircraft closing in leisurely fashion.

"Laura," the captain's voice said in her headset, "target weapons."

"Tracking system engaged," Laura replied, pressing a switch.

"Hold on to your dinner," Chris said.

"I'll do my best," Julie answered. Her fingers tightened around the trigger of the missile launcher.

Donovan and Tyler led their troops toward the edge of the brush that offered them some protection from being sighted. Overhead, the biplane continued its unwavering approach, moving ever closer to the skyfighter.

"Dammit, do something," Donovan whispered through clenched teeth.

Chris felt himself starting to tense, and he ordered his muscles to relax. After all, what was there to get tensed up about? he thought. Just because he had to make a move at the last possible instant before the skyfighter opened fire? If he misjudged, the first shot would blow them out of the sky.

But he had to wait, had to be close enough that the alien craft couldn't match his maneuvers. *Piece of cake . . .*

"Optimum range," Laura said.

"Good," Simon said from the cockpit. "Get it over with—*fire.*"

Now! Chris thought. His hands translated the decision in a split second and the biplane dove down like a rock.

And the laser blast from the Visitor ship sliced through open air where the plane had been a moment earlier.

Simon cursed in his native language.

Donovan and the resistance fighters on the ground wanted to cheer but remained still and silent, watching. Soon, Tyler thought, they'd have to advance.

Inside the stopped Visitor sand rover, Lydia swore to herself.

And Chris let out a war whoop as the Visitor skyfighter, moving too fast to react, flew far past its target and made a steep turn to try another sweep. Chris pulled the plane out of its dive and felt the old girl shudder down to her last rivets. He'd wanted to swing around quickly and give Julie a clear shot at the skyfighter while the Visitors tried to figure out what happened, but the crop duster couldn't respond fast enough. He'd have to be faster himself to compensate.

The skyfighter completed its turn and came straight for them. They wouldn't make the same mistake twice—Chris was sure of that. He guessed they'd try to overwhelm the biplane with a barrage of laser fire, so he threw the plane into a series of aerobatic loops, rolls, and turns, converting them into a very erratically moving target. He also knew they still had one ace up their sleeves—the Visitors didn't know that this little crop duster was armed. The skyfighter momentarily paused after sending several laser blasts increasingly close to them. Chris took advantage of the opportunity and leveled the plane.

"Fire, Julie," he said.

There was no hesitation. Julie's eye aimed through the sight and her finger pressed the trigger. One, two, three— the shells rocketed out of the weapon with surprisingly little recoil. She watched in fascination as they changed course in flight to home in on the Visitor craft.

Simon saw them coming, threw the skyfighter into an evasive dive, and cursed again.

In the weapon turret, Laura whirled her cannon around and took out the first two shells with a curtain of laser bolts.

But the third one found its mark. It hit the skyfighter in one of its maneuvering thruster jets. The initial explosion was just a soft thud. The vessel shivered and then blew up into infinitely small pieces that showered the desert floor, sparkling as they fell. The explosive sound spread rapidly across the open country.

* * *

"*Now*—let's move!" Ham Tyler barked. The resistance squad ran in a spread pattern toward the immobile sand rover.

Inside the rover, Lydia sat stunned. James looked to her for a word, a decision, an order.

Before she could react, the radio chimed with an incoming message. The two Visitors looked at each other. Lydia opened the channel.

"Lydia, you are ordered to surrender your prisoners and your vehicle," said Mike Donovan's voice.

"We have no prisoners, you human slime," Lydia answered. "And you'll pay for the unwarranted destruction of our skyfighter." Then, to James, in a low voice: "Start the engines."

Donovan paused, the radio phone in his hand.

"Look," Tyler said suddenly.

They all saw it—the borer drill on the sand rover's nose had begun to spin. "They're going to try to get away by going down the way they came up," Tyler said.

"Lydia, don't try it," Donovan said. "Our plane is still armed. You try to escape, we'll destroy you before you can get a foot under the sand."

"I don't believe you," Lydia spat.

"Fine—we'll prove it."

On cue, the biplane made a dive and fired a single shell off-target. It hit the ground and blew a plume of dust and dirt a hundred feet up in a minimushroom.

"Better hope they don't call our bluff," Julie said to Chris as he turned the plane away from the sand rover. "I'd hate for them to find out that was our last shell, and it wasn't even a heat-seeker."

"We can't fight like this," Chris said angrily. "We gotta get more weapons through that pipeline."

"I know, I know," Julie said. "Maybe by the time we get back, we'll know something on Ham's Central American connection."

"We better," Chris said, biting off the words.

* * *

"Surrender *now*," Donovan said into the radio phone. "You don't have any choice—except death."

They waited. After a long silence, the Visitor security chief replied, "We're shutting down the vehicle now."

With Ham in the lead, the squad surrounded the sand rover, weapons poised. The side hatch slid open and Lydia stood haughtily in the opening. Unarmed, she climbed out and jumped down to the ground. The three human intelligence agents followed, with James coming out last. Donovan handed the radio phone to Danny and approached Lydia with his laser rifle held ready.

"Well, Mr. Donovan," she said, "I congratulate you on your boldness. This time the day is yours. Or should I say the night. But the victory is only temporary, so savor it. I suppose we're your prisoners?"

Donovan shook his head. "We don't need you as prisoners."

"But we have information." She sounded almost insulted.

"Which we wouldn't get out of you by anything short of torture—and we don't do that, even if it's second nature to you people. And I use *that* word loosely. We don't have prison camps, and we don't eat Visitors—so you're free to go. Besides, I think your going back to face Diana after blowing this mission is more punishment than we could ever inflict on you."

She maintained her silence, lowered her head in a gesture of angry courtesy, and started to climb into the sand rover. Tyler grabbed her arm and roughly pulled her back. "No way, José. You go, this thing stays. If I had my way, lady, we'd take you back and do *something* with you—but I've been outvoted. So why don't you and your friend here just go for a little stroll. Lizards like to walk in the desert at night, don't they?"

There was ice in Tyler's tone, and Lydia straightened, then started walking away. James stood still, and she turned and glared at him. Docilely, he followed his commanding officer, and they headed across the desert without weapons or communications devices.

Two resistance fighters started to climb up into the rover. Tyler turned away from the retreating Visitors, saw them, and let out a roar.

"You idiots! What the hell do you think you're doing?" He yanked them down and shoved them to the ground. "Did it occur to you this thing could be booby-trapped? Or did you think they'd just leave an expensive piece of equipment for us to take joy rides under the desert?"

Sheepishly, the two rebels got to their feet and moved away.

"You really think it's booby-trapped?" Donovan asked Tyler.

"I'd put money on it, but I don't think you want to bet with me again, do you now, Gooder?"

"Okay, let's blow it up."

Ham took a grenade out of his belt pouch, waved to everyone else to move back, pulled the pin, and tossed the grenade inside. Then he dove for cover. The explosion thundered inside the vehicle and a tongue of flame and smoke rolled out the open hatch a few seconds later. The acrid smell of burning plastics wafted on the night breeze. With the trio of liberated prisoners in custody, the resistance squad left the sand rover burning, casting an eerie flickering light on the dark sands.

Chapter 2

Elias Taylor leaned back in the chair at his table in a private corner of Club Creole. The slim black man in his trademark white suit and panama hat surveyed his restaurant and let out a troubled sigh. He'd built this place into Los Angeles' most prestigious spot to see and be seen in the year after the Visitors had been defeated. His sudden fame and status as a heroic freedom fighter had certainly changed his life, and on more than a few nights, he'd pondered the twists of fate that had led to his brother, physician and friend of Julie Parrish, dying in the earliest days of the resistance and his own metamorphosis from small-time hoodlum to rebel to celebrity.

He'd learned a lot about himself—mostly how to turn his talents to legal roads to success. And he'd thought he'd found his path—capitalism and hobnobbing with the beautiful people. To hell with heroism! he'd concluded.

Then the Visitors had returned. The renewed war had nearly destroyed Club Creole before L.A. had been turned into an "open city" following industrialist Nathan Bates's private deal with Diana. Elias' restaurant survived and so did he—but his comfortable acceptance of his new way of upper-class life had suddenly become *un*comfortable. The year he'd come to view as time on *Fantasy Island* looked more and more like a very tenuous existence. There was a real world outside Club Creole's smoked glass, and it needed him. Not as Elias Taylor, restaurateur, but as Elias Taylor, resistance hero. Donovan and Julie and the others had come to him—they needed his help. How could he say no? I tried . . . God, did I try. But in the end, he had had to say yes.

Like others in the resistance, Elias found himself leading a double life. On the one hand was the white-suited host greeting everyone with a smile (just like in *Fantasy Island*), serving the best in food and drink to trendy Angelinos, to officials of Bates's provisional government, even to Visitors in their red uniforms and dark, eye-protecting glasses. The aliens didn't frequent the place, but one of the rules of the city under Nathan Bates was "no discrimination."

Damned lizards even hire me to cater parties at their legation, Elias would think. *As long as they pay me . . .*

But downstairs at Club Creole, Elias ran a whole other establishment. He'd discovered a long-forgotten speakeasy down there, a remnant of Prohibition days. The room's elegance was still intact under years of dust and cobwebs. The ornate, sweeping curves and bold geometry of its Art Deco design still whispered of wealth. He'd planned to open it up as a private club and dining room—until the Visitors came back. Instead, much to Elias' occasional disappointment, the old speakeasy had become a hideaway for the resistance. In a sense, it *was* a place for private meetings, and now it was a haven for the three intelligence agents freed from Lydia's grasp.

With a nod to his maître d', Elias slid out of his chair, disappeared from the main room upstairs, and went through the secret passage in his office. Flashlight in hand, footsteps echoing in the dark, damp corridor, Elias found the stone stairway and descended to his other world.

He emerged into the speakeasy, where his eyes took a second to adjust to the light. When he came down here, he always sighed while he quickly thought of what might have been. *Son of a bitch . . .*

Donovan, Ham Tyler, and Julie were huddled at a marble-topped table.

"How's it goin'?" Elias asked.

"Well," Julie said, "we've figured out how to get

Durning, the American, and Coopersmith, the Brit, back to their territories."

"Okay. How?"

"We marry them off," she said with a grin.

"Huh?" Elias took his hat off and scratched his head.

"They've both gotta go back east," Donovan explained, "so we're going to have them pose as a married couple traveling on our own specially forged travel permits to New York. That's where Durning was working, and Lauren Stewart and Pete Forsythe will be able to get Coopersmith back to England from there."

"Lauren and Pete still working together?" Elias asked. "They sure did a bang-up job with that New York rebel group first time around. But I got one big question."

"What's that?" Julie asked.

Elias raised his hands. "I just gotta picture this. See, I've *seen* Durning and Coopersmith. Durning looks like a bus driver and Coopersmith looks like a *Playboy* Bunny. Who's gonna believe they're married? I mean, what would be in it for her?"

"He's great in bed," Ham said.

"You CIA guys would know," Elias said with a shrug. "But what about the Japanese dude?"

"That's more of a problem," Julie said.

"Why?" Elias asked. "I mean, can't we ship him home right from here?"

"Yeah," Julie continued, "except that in New York, because the red dust works there, it's Earth-controlled territory. So once we get Durning and Coopersmith there, they're home free. But, except for L.A. being Bates-controlled territory, most of the West Coast is Visitor dominated. We've got to figure out a way to get him out of the country. It would be great if we could fly him out, but the Visitors' patrols make that too risky."

"Now that you're through retelling the Bible," Ham said, "are you ready to hear the plan I got worked out?"

"Sure, since you asked so politely," Julie said.

Ham gave her a dirty look. "It's not so tough. We've got some resistance people up the coast. We've also got a few

Navy subs patrolling the coast. We sneak Maragato up to one of these fishing villages, take him out on a fishing boat, and once we're out in the ocean where the Visitors and Nathan Bates's spies aren't, we transfer him to the sub. They sail to Japan, and *voilà!*—he's home." Tyler looked at his colleagues for reaction. For several long moments, there wasn't any as they chewed over his idea. He drummed his fingers impatiently. "Well? It's a simple plan—there's not that much to think about."

Donovan raised his eyebrows. "It *is* a simple plan, relatively speaking. I hate to say it, but I think we should go with it."

"Don't bowl me over with your enthusiasm," Ham growled.

Diana's real eyes burned their angriest red; her human-eye contacts were out, sitting in their container on her cabin countertop.

"You found them *where*?" she said to the intercom.

"Wandering in the desert outside of Los Angeles," a male voice said from the speaker. "They're being flown back to the Mother Ship now, Diana."

"I want to see them, Captain."

"I thought you would. I've given orders that Lydia and James should report to you as soon as they've had a chance to change into fresh uniforms."

"I want to see them immediately, Captain. I don't care if they're dirty, hot, and tired. They report to me the *instant* they set foot aboard this ship. Is that clear? If there's any delay whatsoever, you will be held responsible."

"Yes, Diana. As soon as they come aboard." His voice betrayed fear now. "I'll see to it myself."

"Good," Diana said sweetly. "I'm counting on you."

As ordered, Lydia and James were hustled directly to the supreme commander's quarters. Their uniforms were tattered and dusty from a day and night of traversing rugged desert terrain. The hot, dry air had even caused some cracking in their bioplastic skins. Diana made them stand at attention as she circled them.

"We are fighting for our very survival here," she said, in a perfectly controlled voice. She was enjoying Lydia's discomfort too much to allow her own fury to dilute the moment of dominance. "We have no room for extreme incompetence of the sort you two displayed in this incident. There'll obviously be a full investigation by a command tribunal—charges may be brought at any time. But I have questions of my own right now. Why didn't you have more backup than a single skyfighter?"

Lydia broke her face-front pose to glare at Diana. "It was your order to minimize the amount of personnel used for this phase of the mission. You complained about how much time and energy we were wasting tracking these human spies down and capturing them."

"I do not *complain*, Lydia. I *command*—or have you forgotten that? James, you're dismissed. Consider yourself on probation. If I were you, I'd be extremely careful what I do until the tribunal investigation is complete."

He nodded curtly and left the room. Lydia started to slump her shoulders and Diana snapped a sharp look at her. "You are still at attention, Lydia." Diana placed her hands on her hips, then abruptly turned and sat in a lounge chair, reclining, a purposeful contrast with Lydia's formal posture. "I could have you executed for this bungling, but I won't. I need you too much. But I don't want any misunderstanding, Lydia. If you ever commit another error of this magnitude, I'll do everything I can to destroy your career—and I can do a lot, Commander. I can also take your life any time I choose. Dismissed."

Without a word, Lydia marched out. Diana knew the security chief was seething, and when her door slid shut, the supreme commander allowed herself a cold smile.

James sat on his bunk, his dirty uniform stripped off. He'd had a lot of time to think about things while walking in that forsaken desert. He and Lydia hadn't talked much during their trek back to the nearest Visitor outpost. He was a young officer with high hopes for his future. He'd cast his lot with Lydia because he believed her to be more pragmatic and less volatile than Diana. Had he made a mistake?

His door chimed and he pressed a button to open it. Lydia, still in her torn uniform, stepped in and the hatch closed behind her. She took a deep breath. "We've had better days, eh, James?"

He managed a smile and motioned her over to the bed. She came to him and their arms closed around each other. They kissed, their long reptilian tongues intertwining, clashing playfully, then drawing back. He began to unsnap her uniform fastenings and slid it off her shoulders. He trailed kisses down her face to her neck and shoulders. It had taken some time to get used to making love to a human body, but it wasn't so bad now. The human shape and the simulated skin had a certain pleasurable softness their own bodies lacked.

"I'm not going to let Diana get away with this humiliation of us," Lydia purred, her breathing becoming quicker as James caressed her. "We're going to strike back, solidify our own power. Maybe I'll even replace her as supreme commander."

That made James pause, and his eyes met hers questioningly. "What are you talking about?"

Lydia smiled, pleased that she had his attention in more ways than one. "I'm talking about something spectacular, something bold. But I'll need you with me." She stood and slipped her uniform off. As it fell to the floor, she reached over to dim the lights.

"I'm always with you—you know that," he said as she lay back on the bed next to him.

She raised her eyebrows tolerantly. "Are you? Sometimes I wonder. You're a mercenary at heart, James. So am I. Maybe that's why we work so well together. It doesn't really matter, though. If I'm successful, we'll be successful together."

"Just what do you have in mind?" he asked, his fingers tracing lightly from her shoulder down over her breasts, past the curve of her hip.

"What do I have in mind? Nothing less than the capture

of one of our most formidable enemies, one of the humans Diana hates the most—*Michael Donovan*."

James smiled. "Oh, I'm with you, Lydia."

Their reptilian tongues snaked out sensuously and their mouths met in a deep kiss.

Chapter 3

Downstairs at Club Creole, Donovan spread the California map out as Tyler, Chris, and the others gathered around. "Okay, here's the plan. We've got people in a little town out near San Luis Obispo."

"North of Vandenberg Air Force Base?" Ham Tyler said.

Donovan nodded. "Yeah. It's called Castillo Beach. It's so small, it's not even on the map." He stopped and glanced around. "Hey, where's Julie?"

The door to the secret corridor swung in and Julie rushed over to them, breathless and grinning. "Hi, sorry I'm late. I've got great news!" she blurted.

"What news?" Donovan said.

"Elias just gave me the message. Ham's Central American connection is coming through with a heavy shipment of weapons and ammunition for us!"

The group burst into cheers, and Julie held her hands up for attention. "We've got Uzis, more heat-seeking shells and launchers, lots of Teflon-coated bullets—the works! It'll be coming by boat. We don't know exactly when or where, just that it'll be in the next couple of days and it'll be on the coast just south of San Clemente."

"Ah, yes, good old San Clemency," Donovan said with a reminiscing smile.

"Huh?" Julie said.

"That's what we called the place when Richard Nixon still lived there after he got pardoned by Jerry Ford back in 'seventy-four, after Watergate."

"Whoa," Tyler said. "Maybe that's what you pinko liberals in the media called it, but some of us more patriotic types had a little more respect for the Commander-in-Chief."

"I wasn't in the pinko liberal media back then," Donovan countered. "I was a student—"

"Ah-*ha*!" Tyler interrupted.

"—and a *little* respect is more than the man deserved!"

Julie couldn't help laughing. It happened to be great fun to watch Donovan and Tyler argue, but this wasn't the time. She waved her arms emphatically. "Ancient history, guys! We've got details to work out here"—she saw the map— "which I see you've already started."

"Actually," Donovan said, "we were working out how to get Maragato back to Japan. Your little piece of news may mean splitting our manpower and doing both at once."

"We should be able to swing it," Tyler said, "if we get everybody pitching in. Right, Elias, my man?"

He turned to glare pointedly at Elias Taylor, who'd brought Julie down and was now hanging back near the exit.

"Hey, man," Elias protested, "I got a restaurant to run. I got people expectin' me to be upstairs when they come to hobnob with the rich and powerful—people like Nathan Bates."

"Speaking of shit-for-brains Bates," Tyler said, "where's that kid of his?"

"I know where he is," Chris said.

"Go get him," Tyler said. "I've got an assignment for the two of you."

"You want him, you got him," Chris said amiably. He headed for the door.

The trail bike jumped up over the hillock and skidded for a perilous moment as its wheels hit the grass. But Kyle Bates handled his favorite mode of transportation with the skill of a jockey on a thoroughbred. Behind him on the seat, Elizabeth Maxwell sat pressed against his back, her arms locked around his waist as she screamed with a combination of fear and glee. Her blond hair whipped in the wind. Kyle steered the bike toward a wood-fenced corral and braked to a gentle halt. The pair of horses inside the enclosure moved away to graze at a safe distance from the noisy new arrivals.

"Hey, you don't have to squash me!" Kyle said in mock anger.

Elizabeth didn't catch the humor. She broke the embrace and recoiled as if she'd done something awful. "I—I'm sorry."

Kyle turned and grinned. "Hey, I was just kidding." He wiped the beads of sweat off his handsome face. Elizabeth slid off the bike and wandered toward the corral. Kyle stood for a moment, not following, just watching.

Elizabeth, the star child, he thought. She looked like any other pretty eighteen-year-old girl. But of course she wasn't just another teenager, she was a hybrid—part Visitor, part human. Ever since he'd met her, Kyle had wondered just how much she was of each—and what did the total add up to? And he had to keep reminding himself that she might physically look like a full-grown woman, but she was really only eighteen *months* old! She was brilliant beyond measuring, she had some pretty strange psychic powers that Julie was still trying to catalogue, but she'd only been born a scant year and a half ago—and her life had hardly been normal. So Kyle knew he had to be extra careful with the way he treated her. She wasn't just another girl to be taken to dinner and then to bed. Not that he wasn't physically attracted to her. He'd been disappointed when she quickly broke the bear hug on the bike. But he also felt like a big brother to her. He wanted to show her some of his world, share it with her. He knew she felt as if she didn't belong, didn't fit in, and he'd always felt the same way. That sense of alienation had been even worse since the Visitors had come back and his father had struck his deal with Diana— becoming, in many eyes, the most brazen human collaborator on the planet.

Kyle had thought of changing his name. He and his father had been fighting since Kyle was a kid anyway. This was just the latest in a long line of last straws. But he'd settled for having nothing at all to do with the old man and becoming a sometime resistance fighter.

Since meeting Elizabeth by accident one day at Club Creole, he'd been spending more time with the underground group as an excuse to be near her, and he'd won permission to be alone with her, even take her away from resistance headquarters, as long as someone knew where they were going. Kyle was only too aware that Diana badly wanted to get Elizabeth back under her control, to see what her bioengineering experiment had wrought. Kyle found himself feeling fiercely protective when it came to Elizabeth's safety. Even out here he was always alert for any sign of trouble.

He finally joined her at the corral. Both horses had come over to her, and she petted them and fed them handfuls of long hay from bales just outside the fence.

"Where are we, Kyle?"

"My dad owns this land, but don't worry. He never comes up here."

"Then why does he own it?"

Kyle shrugged. "I think he's saving it for me. You know, sort of a bribe to make me be the kind of kid he wants me to be. I'm a good boy, and he gives me the land."

"Do you want it?"

"Not like that," Kyle said, looking into her eyes. "Did you have fun on the bike?"

"I was scared sometimes."

"But I heard you laughing sometimes too. I think it's the first time I've ever seen you laugh."

"Sometimes I laugh," she said with a defensive pout.

"Not often enough—but you're getting better. I know it hasn't been easy for you, but you know we all care about you—a lot."

"I know," she said softly. "You're the first friends I've ever had. I think it's getting easier to feel like you won't all go away and leave me, or that the Visitors won't kill you all."

He hugged her impulsively. Tentatively, she hugged him

back. "We're not gonna leave you," he whispered. "And we won't let the Visitors get you, that's for sure."

The sound of a motor caught his ear and he whirled to search for the source. Down the hillside, he spotted a tiny dust plume approaching. As it got closer, it resolved into a man on a motorcycle—Chris. He skidded to a stop a few yards away.

"Hey, they want you back at the club," Chris called. "You didn't ride all the way up here on that itty-bitty bike, did you?"

"No," Kyle said. "I've got my Blazer." He pointed to the four-wheel drive parked nearby in the shade of a tall tree.

"Okay, let's move out then," Chris said.

Nathan Bates never tired of the panoramic view from his office in the high-rise headquarters of Science Frontiers, once simply his corporate empire and now the seat of Los Angeles' tenuous provisional government. He stood at the expanse of glass, tinted just enough to cut down the heat of the California sun but not enough to alter the brilliant colors of sunrise or sunset.

Back in the simpler days when he'd been chief executive of the company he'd built into one of the world's most successful and innovative scientific, research, and development entities, he'd found he needed to have those two times a day set aside for meditation, silence, and solitude. He'd arrive early to watch the sun come up before any of his employees got in. And if he was still working at sunset, he would order his office cleared so he could watch the day end.

Now, with the very survival of the planet partly in his hands, he needed those quiet moments even more. He needed to wrestle with his own thoughts, sort them out, place them in perspective, and he needed to observe something made by God, not by Nathan Bates.

He often wondered what the outcome of his agreement with Diana would be. When the deal was struck, he really hadn't thought much past the moment. And what a moment it was. . . .

Diana had led the Visitors back to take another shot at destroying Earth. Bates had discovered that the red-dust toxin Science Frontiers had helped develop and manufacture wasn't going to save humankind after all. It worked in some areas of the globe, but not in others. The military situation was critical. *We were losing,* Bates thought now. *We were on the brink.*

He'd had Diana in his hands, and she'd escaped. And when she saw him again, it was she who was holding all the high cards—except one: he threatened to fill L.A.'s air with a massive dose of the toxin that might not last long, but would kill every Visitor in the vicinity. So they'd agreed to a peace of sorts, a local peace while the war raged elsewhere in the world. And Bates was potentate here. What he did, how he dealt with Diana, could prolong the human world, save it, or destroy it.

"Nathan."

He turned slowly to see Julie Parrish, wearing a denim skirt and her white lab coat. Only a few years older than Kyle, Julie was young enough to be his daughter, but his feelings toward her were definitely not of the fatherly variety. Not that he'd done anything about the situation yet. But he would, when the time was right. For now, Julie was still one of his top scientists.

"Yes, Julie, what is it?"

She looked confused. "That's what I came to ask you. I got a memo that you wanted to see me."

"Oh, that's right. I've been preoccupied lately."

"Anything I can help you with?"

He smiled. "No, no, it's—"

He was cut off by the chiming of his intercom. He reached across the massive desk and touched a button. "Yes?"

"Sorry to disturb you, sir," said his secretary, Caroline, "but Diana is on the tie line. She wants to talk to you—*now.*"

Julie started for the door of the plush office, but Bates

waved her to a seat. "Stay. Okay, Caroline, I'll take it." He sat back in his tall leather chair and touched another button on the desk-top control panel. A section of the wall slid aside to reveal a large video screen. He punched in the line code and Diana's chilly features appeared on the screen.

Every time she saw that face, Julie's blood ran cold. No matter how she tried to fight the reaction, she couldn't help it—couldn't forget the tortures she'd endured as a prisoner on Diana's ship almost two years ago, as a victim of the Visitors' demonic conversion process. She'd survived it, but not without psychic scars, and the shivers she felt seeing Diana life-size, even on a TV screen—that was something she'd just have to live with.

"How nice to see you, Nathan," Diana said smoothly. "And you too, Dr. Parrish."

"What can I do for you, Diana?" Bates asked.

"I have an urgent matter to discuss with you."

Bates spread his hands. "Go right ahead."

"In person only," Diana said. "To make it easier for you, we could meet right in Los Angeles, at our legation building. Unless you'd prefer to meet up here in my ship."

"No, thank you, Diana. Here would be fine. Space flight makes me queasy. First thing tomorrow?"

Diana dropped her pretense at charm. "No. Immediately."

"Why now? Surely it can wait—"

"No, it can't wait. The consequences of waiting could be more than you bargain for."

Bates smiled. "Why, Diana, is that a threat?"

She returned his smile. "Yes, that's exactly what it is. I'll see you in thirty minutes."

"Thirty minutes it is," Bates said.

The screen went blank and Bates touched the switch to close the wall panel.

"Are you going?" Julie asked.

Bates shrugged. "It didn't sound as if I have a lot of choice, did it?"

Julie got up and came over to his desk. "How can you be

sure she hasn't decided your agreement doesn't suit her needs anymore?"

"I can't be, but I appreciate your concern, Julie." He reached out and took her hand in his as she sat on the edge of the desk. "I just have to trust my judgment and timing. I'd like to think I can outguess her. Maybe *I'll* break the deal first and take the advantage. Diana and I are playing Russian roulette. It's a power game—the most exciting game of all."

"But the stakes include the fate of the world and four billion people."

He nodded. "All the more reason why I won't make a mistake. It's not just my neck on the line. Oh, I know the people you were in the resistance with don't believe I've got any interests at heart other than my own, but that's just not true, Julie." He patted her hand, somehow combining reassurance and affection in the gesture.

Julie watched Bates's gray Lincoln limo pull away from the building, then walked slowly across the parking lot to her own Mazda RX-7. One of these days Bates was going to make a pass at her—she was sure of that. She wasn't so sure of how she'd react. He *was* attractive, and she was more than a little annoyed at herself to find she wasn't immune to the sex appeal of power and wealth. And while she didn't agree with much of what Bates did in his relations with Diana, neither did she agree with the totally negative opinions of Bates shared by most of her fellow underground members. His treaty *had* preserved a semblance of life and had bought time for humanity to catch its breath and gird for the long fight.

What *was* Bates's ultimate goal? Was it conquest of the world, with himself as ruler? She didn't really know. It wasn't in her realm of experience to imagine that any person could actually think in those terms. *He's not Hitler or Napoleon,* she mused.

She unlocked the car door and slid in. Bates had thought she was concerned for his safety when she questioned his meeting with Diana. Not that she didn't care what happened to him—she'd already saved his life once when Ham Tyler had set up an assassination attempt—but she was considerably more preoccupied by what the meeting meant in terms of what Diana might be up to.

At times like these, knowing how Bates felt about her, Julie became acutely uncomfortable with her double life—being Bates's employee by day and a resistance fighter whenever necessary. She started the car and drove out the guarded gates of Science Frontiers.

The immense gray limousine pulled into the circular drive in front of the Visitor legation. Only a couple of years ago, this building was the Soviet Embassy. The irony of swapping one "evil empire" for another always prodded a half smile from Bates. He finished his Scotch on the rocks, put the glass on the limo's bar, and slid the small divider open so he could see the driver. "Wait for me. I don't know how long I'll be."

Bates opened the rear door and stepped out into the fading daylight. Two Visitor guards in standard red uniforms and dark glasses came down the steps to escort him inside.

Boot heels clicked on the marble floor, and Bates had to walk quickly to keep up. He glanced at the Visitor flags and banners around the foyer. The new occupants seemed to share the Soviet taste for cool functionality and had a similar obsession with symbols of identity and power. The guards led him to Diana's office, where two other guards opened the doors and let him in.

Diana wasn't at her desk, but in a comfortable chair off to the side. She remained seated and imperiously nodded for Bates to join her. A bottle of fine wine from the supply left behind by the Russians waited with a pair of glasses on a tray.

"Something to drink, Mr. Bates?"

"Don't mind if I do."

"Then pour it."

Bates knew the ploy. She refused to play hostess, and his pouring the wine cast him in the role of inferior. He'd never met with Diana without going through a similar routine, establishing his status in her eyes.

He didn't care. The wine was an excellent vintage and he really did want some. He'd spent a lifetime studying the psychology of opponents, but they'd all been human. This was an intriguing change of pace.

"Would you care for some, Diana?"

"Thank you."

He poured two glasses and passed one to her. "Picking up human vices, are we?"

She smiled, ice in her eyes. "Not at all."

"I'd love to chitchat the evening away, but that's not why I'm here. Why don't you get to the point?"

"Fine," she said, taking a sip. "The point is this. When we reached our treaty agreement, you swore to keep Los Angeles and the surrounding area under control, and totally demilitarized."

"And we're doing our best."

"Your best isn't good enough, Mr. Bates," Diana said sharply. "Los Angeles is both a conduit and a destination point for entirely too much weaponry being used against our forces."

"Look, Diana, there's an angry world out there, with people being killed by Visitors. And that means not everyone here is going to love you. I have limited resources. I can't stop every bullet or pistol from being used to kill Visitors."

"I think you can do more than you've been doing, and if you don't start, I'll be forced to take actions you may not like."

Bates spread his hands. "If you want to increase your patrols outside my borders, be my guest."

"That's already being done. And I don't need your permission for it. But that's not what I'm warning you about."

"What, then?"

"I'll make it clear, Mr. Bates. If you don't stop the weapons being supplied to the supposedly outlawed rebel group in your provisional zone, I'll have no choice but to assume that you aren't really interested in coexistence, I'll consider our treaty abrogated, and I'll do something I've wanted to do for a very long time—I'll level your precious city.''

Bates gripped the stem of the wineglass tightly—he hoped Diana didn't notice. He did *not* want to lose his temper with her. "This is a very serious threat, Diana. You're aware I couldn't stand by and let you carry it out."

"Oh, you'd have very little choice."

"There's still the red toxin. I can still unleash our supply and you couldn't stop it."

"I'd be willing to take that risk. We'd lose some territory and some soldiers, but it's a big world out there and I'd be willing to conquer some of it and leave Los Angeles to you. The survivors might not fare well in radioactive rubble, but the city would be yours. Think about it, Mr. Bates. But don't think too long. If I don't see some results in a week, I'll carry out my threat."

Bates finished his wine, put the glass down, and stood. "Good-bye, Diana. Enjoy the wine."

Chapter 4

Elias lifted his wineglass. "Here's to the happy wedding couple. May the union be short and sweet—and safe!"

The group of resistance members gathered downstairs at Club Creole clinked their glasses together with a chorus of "Amens!" and "Cheers!" as they drank to the imminent departure of Dave Durning and Susan Coopersmith, who sat in the middle of the party.

"What time do you hit the road?" Elias asked.

"Eight in the morning," Coopersmith said. "If only my mum were here to warn me about the wedding night," she added with mock concern.

"Will you be able to support me in the style to which I've been accustomed?" asked the easygoing Durning, his round face lit with a gentle smile.

"First class all the way—at least until I ditch you in New York."

Someone in the back began to sing, "I wanna be around to pick up the pieces when somebody breaks your heart. . . ."

"Hey, this ain't gonna be a cakewalk back east, folks," Ham Tyler said sourly. "Forged papers or no, the Visitors sometimes make up the rules as they go along. You can wear a beard and hairpiece, Dave, and we can make you up to be an ugly broad, Suzie—"

"Nobody could do that," Donovan cut in lightly as Julie socked him on the shoulder, then snuggled close to him.

The group laughed, but Tyler shook his head. "Joke all you want, Gooder. Disguises might not be enough to save their hides is all I'm saying."

Maggie Blodgett, the pretty blond who was the rebels' best pilot, draped an arm over Ham's shoulders. "You're so much fun at parties, Mr. Tyler."

"Yeah, ease up, Ham," Elias said.

Tyler disengaged himself from Maggie. "Go ahead, get cocky. See if I care. But when you screw up because of it, don't come crying to me."

He turned to find a corner by himself, but Chris came up to him and said, "Gotta talk, Ham." They sat down a distance from the party.

"What's up, Chris?"

"Somethin's not right about Maragato."

Ham glanced furtively over his shoulder at the Japanese agent chatting with some of the underground members across the room.

"What do you mean?"

Chris sipped his beer. "You know him, right?"

"Yeah, our paths have crossed before."

"I remember you tellin' me about a brouhaha you had with him and the Japanese government over a Korean pilot who defected with one of those new MiGs."

"Yeah, I happened to be the guy who found him when he landed in South Korea. The Japs sent Maragato over to look the plane over and debrief the guy. It so happens Maragato speaks Korean and I don't. We worked real closely, you might say—fought over every little thing and wound up hating each other. So what else is new?"

"Yeah, well, he doesn't recall any of that," Chris said quietly.

Ham narrowed his eyes. "You sure?"

"Positive. I talked to the guy for a while after Kyle and me came back here today. From time to time, I looked into his eyes and got a real strong feelin' there was nobody home. But then he'd seem fine. That's when I brought up his run-in with you."

"And he didn't remember it? Damn, when I ream a guy

out like I did to him, I'd really like to be remembered for it. Maybe he just didn't want to talk about it—you know how they can be about saving face."

Chris shook his head. "Nah, I think it was more than that. I really think he didn't recall it at all. I thought you should know."

Ham scratched his face absently. "Hmm, you think Diana's already screwed around with those little mind tricks of hers?"

"That's the first thing I thought of. But then why was he included in on this deal with Lydia? Think Diana's got something else in mind? Would she trick her own security chief?"

"Maybe Lydia's the one playing the tricks," Ham said.

"On Diana?"

"Could be. Wouldn't be the first time. Those two ladies aren't real fond of each other."

Chris finished his mug of beer. "If Maragato's already been converted, he could've been planted as a sort of counterspy. Maybe Lydia planned to *let* us get these three back from her."

Tyler nodded. "Maybe our wedding couple's not for real either. Did you notice anything about them?"

Chris shook his head. "But that don't really mean anything. Maybe I should blow Maragato away, just to be on the safe side. Make it look like an accident."

"No, let's wait and see. We know to keep an eye on him, so I don't think it can get too far out of hand."

"You sure, Ham? Just bringing him here to the club's already got us in trouble—if he's a Visitor spy and he gets away from us, that is."

"Donovan was responsible for bringing him here. If it turns out Maragato's one nonkosher Jap, it could be just the ammo I need to knock Donovan out of the box and run this show myself. Keep it under your hat for now—and keep your eyes open." Tyler scanned the crowd for Kyle Bates and spotted him sitting in a booth with Elizabeth Maxwell. "Kyle and the lizard kid are getting pretty tight, eh, Chris?"

"I wouldn't worry about it. A little young love never killed anybody."

"I wouldn't know, Chris, I wouldn't know. Hey, Kyle—over here, kid."

Kyle told Elizabeth to wait, then came over to Ham and Chris. "Yeah, what is it, Tyler?"

"Got a job for you two tomorrow. Sit down."

Kyle did as he was told, crossing his arms sullenly. "What?"

"This Japanese guy, Maragato—we want to ship him out to sea by boat. I want you two to ride out to a little fishing town called Castillo Beach, make contact with some of our people up there, tell 'em what we've got in mind, and make sure they can come through."

Kyle thought for a moment. "Take a ride up the coast? Shouldn't be too bad. What time?"

"Dawn," Tyler said. "So don't let the lizard kid keep you up too late."

Kyle stiffened. "Don't call her that," he said tightly.

Ham raised his hands. "Hey, sorry, kid. Just don't want to see you in over your head."

Kyle shoved the chair back, banging it into the wall. "That's my problem. I don't have to listen to crap like that from my father, and I certainly don't have to take it from you."

Ham watched with an amused half smile as Kyle stalked angrily back to the star child across the room. "Sensitive, isn't he?"

Chris shrugged his broad shoulders. "Give him a break, Ham. He's not a bad kid."

"He doesn't like to listen. That could cause trouble some time when we just don't need it."

"You made me his baby-sitter—you let me worry about it."

"Love to, Chris. But you may not always be there to save his skin."

The next morning dawned hot and clear in Los Angeles. Chris and Kyle mounted their motorcycles and headed north up the coast. While Julie went to work at Science Frontiers, Tyler and Donovan met with others of the resistance to plan strategy. Ham's Central American contacts had radioed during the night—the weapons shipment would arrive in two days. Tyler answered:*"We'll be there."*

"I don't like it," Donovan said as they checked the maps in Club Creole's lower level.

"I don't like it either, Gooder, but we haven't got a hell of a lot of choice. We've got two things to do at once, so we split up our people and do 'em—the faster the better. You, me, and Chris should be enough to get Maragato up to Castillo Beach. Julie can lead another bunch to pick up the weapons. She's done this sort of thing before."

"Why can't you go with Julie and I take Maragato?"

"I got my reasons for wanting to go along up north."

Donovan frowned. "Yeah, that's what I'm afraid of. I want to know those reasons."

"I like the climate there better," Tyler said sarcastically.

Elizabeth wandered over to the planning session. "Can I go with Julie?" she asked shyly.

"I think it's better if you don't, Elizabeth," Donovan said. "It's safer for you here. Especially with your mom away. Robin would be very unhappy if we didn't take good care of you."

"But I want to feel like I'm helping. Everyone's always protecting me."

"Hell, Donovan, let the kid go. It shouldn't be too dangerous a mission, and I'll send the Bates kid along. He'll look after her."

Donovan glared at Tyler, then said to Elizabeth, "We'll think about it."

By midday, Chris and Kyle had returned to the speakeasy after wending their way through a maze of passageways under the streets from several blocks away. They met Ham and Donovan inside.

"Got a few changes in the plan," Chris reported.

"Like what?" Ham asked.

"Talked to Art Grant—he's the skipper of the fishing

boat, the *Pegasus*. He loved the idea of getting Maragato out to the sub. He's worked with the Navy before, and he'll make the arrangements with them, no sweat.''

"So what's different?'' Donovan said.

"They don't want us to take the risk of traveling along the coast,'' Chris continued. "Two reasons—there's a lot more Visitor patrols in that area and Grant wouldn't want us to have to run that gauntlet. He also doesn't want us to lead any tricky Visitors to them by accident.''

"So what do we do instead?'' Donovan asked, annoyance evident in his tone.

"Indirect transfer,'' Kyle said.

Chris nodded. "They gave coordinates for a place up in the mountains. Gimme the map.''

Donovan unfolded the map and spread it out on a table. Chris bent low, moving his finger carefully along. "It's in the Panza range.''

"What's the nearest town?'' Ham asked.

"Santa Margarita,'' Chris said, "but we're not talking next door, Ham. I'm lookin' for a place called Crow's Fork. It's so tiny, it ain't even on a map—and the place you're supposed to meet Grant's people is a couple of miles outside *that*. Here we go—off Route 58.'' Chris put his fingertip on the spot. Donovan and Tyler peered at it, then at each other—then at Chris.

"Major metropolitan area,'' Donovan deadpanned. "Still, from their point of view, I guess they're right.''

"They gave me directions to an old mine outside of Crow's Fork,'' Chris said. He pulled a piece of paper out of the pocket of his denim jacket and handed it to Donovan, but Tyler snatched it first. Donovan glared.

Ham shrugged. "I know that area a little. It's real rugged, Gooder. We did some maneuvers up there, and we're not going to be able to drive up.''

"Even in a four-by-four?''

Tyler shook his head. "Horseback or foot. I vote for the horses.''

Donovan's mouth tightened. "Where the hell are we going to get horses up there in the middle of nowhere?''

"Just so happens I know some trail guides up there," Ham said. "One of 'em worked with the Company a little in Central America a couple of years ago. I was part of that job."

"You sure they'll remember you?" Donovan said.

"Oh, they'll remember," Ham said with a mysterious half smile. "They'll remember. Okay, then—Chris, you're going to make this trip with me and Donovan. Kid," he said to Kyle, "you're going to head south with Julie and back her up on the weapons pickup. You and Chris keep bitching about his baby-sitting you—well, you're going to be on your own. You blow it, you'll regret it. You do what Julie says—she's in charge down there."

Kyle cocked his head. "What d'you want, a salute?"

"Not from you, kid."

Barry walked along the catwalk above the Mother Ship's hangar deck. His human contours conformed to those of his own reptilian body—short and stocky—and certain narrow sections of the catwalk were a squeeze for him. He wondered if Donovan and the humans had managed to get the liberated intelligence agents to safety yet. As long as they were anywhere near Los Angeles, he expected Lydia and Diana to be exerting extra efforts to recapture them. It was sometimes the fate of fifth columnists like himself to remain in the dark as to how helpful they'd actually been to the humans fighting the Visitor reinvasion. He reached a ladder, hauled himself up, and emerged into a main ship's corridor. The junior officer on guard duty, in full body armor, saluted him.

"May I see your security clearance, Captain?" the young female guard asked.

"Is this part of Lydia's new procedure, Lieutenant?" He reached into a pocket and pulled out his ID card.

She inserted it into a square scanning device the size of a deck of cards. It flashed yellow, then green. She handed the card back. "Yes, sir," she said. "It's been a lot of extra work for us, but I suppose there's a lot at stake."

Barry nodded. "That there is. Carry on, Lieutenant."

She saluted and he moved on. The crackdown had made things uncomfortable for the fifth columnists, he thought. There'd been no direct contact with the resistance since Lydia and James had lost the prisoners and returned to face Diana's fury. If anything important came up now, it might be impossible to help the humans without risking revelation of the secret Visitor network sworn to help the people of Earth.

Deep inside the massive Mother Ship over Los Angeles, Lydia entered the security computer section. Its entry corridor had three sets of code-locked doors, and only crew members with special clearance knew the three codes to be punched into the digital pads on the wall.

Lydia tapped in the final numbers and the last set of doors parted to allow her to enter. She nodded a silent greeting to Barry, already working at a console, and proceeded to her private cubicle in the corner. Halfway across the dimly lit room, she stopped.

"Barry, I'd like to discuss something with you."

He switched his terminal to standby mode and came over to her work station. She gestured toward an extra seat, and he took it.

"Yes, Lydia?"

She took a deep, dramatic breath. "When I handpicked you for this section, I had every reason to believe you'd become a valuable asset to me, Captain."

Barry lowered his head in self-deprecation. "I hope I've lived up to your expectations."

"Oh, you have—and more. That's why I'm trusting you with information no one else can know about. Now, then— you're probably well aware of my recent run-in with Diana over the loss of those three human prisoners. Your work in correlating information was one of the key components in our successfully capturing them in the first place. I blame Diana's misallocation of manpower for our eventual failure. And I aim to reestablish the honor of fleet security. We've all been tainted by this incident, and we don't deserve it."

"Do you have a plan in mind, Commander?"

She nodded. "Yes, I certainly do. Diana is too foolish to

ever attempt anything as bold as this. She's too wrapped up in her power games with Nathan Bates. We don't have time for that—we've got a mission to accomplish on this planet, a mission for the Great Leader. When he sent us here, he didn't plan for Diana to be in charge. Now that she is, there's nothing he can do about it."

Barry smiled. "But we can?"

"Exactly. I like the way you think, Barry. I've created a basic strategy, but I'll need you to work out the details and make it work. I can't think of anyone who's more skilled at this than you."

"Thank you, Lydia. I must say you've piqued my curiosity. What's your idea?"

She touched several keys on her computer panel. The screen flashed a global map of the planet Earth turning on its axis, looking as it would from space. Red covered the land masses dominated by Visitor forces—areas where the weather was warm all year, making the red-dust toxin ineffective for more than one annual life cycle. Barry wondered fleetingly who had been more surprised to discover that the bacteria in the toxin needed a dormant cold-weather season to flourish and reproduce—the invaders or the humans who'd created the deadly stuff. No matter—

Yellow filled in the countries under human control, and Lydia froze the graphic with the continent of North America centered on the screen. "As you can see," she said, "most of the industrialized world has a winter season, making it very difficult for us to dominate those variable climate zones. But much of the United States is now toxin free— and we know that the U.S. is the most powerful nation on earth. If we could conquer the warm parts of this continent, we would have a very real chance to finish off all resistance, or at least force humanity to kneel to us and beg for peace on *our* terms. Do you agree?"

"Yes, but how do we do that?"

"I have a plan to disrupt electrical power across America. Deprived of power, the humans would be at a distinct disadvantage. Their computers, their manufacturing facilities, much of their communications system—none of it would work without electricity."

"Are you sure we could disrupt the whole national power grid?"

"That's your job—to tell me if it's possible. I think it is. I did some preliminary research and found that they've had major blackouts—that's what they call them—which have cut off power to vast sections of the industrialized nations. With our resources, we should be able to cause such results from coast to coast."

"But much of their communications equipment can be run by generators or batteries."

"Not if we detonate a small number of nuclear warheads high overhead. It'll cause an electromagnetic pulse that will disrupt all communications without exception. Then we can invade the continent under cover of night and chaos. Fallout will be minimal."

Barry was silent—*Lydia's plan might just work!* He made an effort to look fascinated, not horrified, by what he'd just heard.

"Well, what do you think?" she prodded.

"It could work," he said honestly, noncommittally. "Would you like me to get to work on it right away?"

"Yes. Here's the preliminary strategy," she said, handing him a small cassette. "You'll need this to get into the bank containing my research. It's under exclusive security lock, and this cassette is the only key that can unlock it. Don't lose it," she said with a cold smile.

She pushed back her chair and stood, and Barry got to his feet to return to his own work console. "When do you want a report, Lydia?"

"By the start of the next duty shift. You have seven hours. I suggest you get to work."

When she was gone, Barry allowed himself to feel stunned for the first time. Somehow he had to contact Donovan!

Chapter 5

Julie slipped her lab coat off and hung it over her desk chair. The grumble in her stomach told her she should have taken a lunch break at least an hour ago, but her current bioresearch project was nearing the stage where she hated to leave it for such mundane needs as sleeping and eating. She glanced briefly at the small, framed snapshot of Mike Donovan next to her phone and realized she might make an exception where sex was concerned, but all she could muster now was a longing sigh. She and Mike hadn't had much time for their personal lives lately. She thought back to their excited discussions of building a life together after the Visitors had been driven from the planet the first time, but somehow her life never worked out that simply. *Really horrible things don't usually happen to me*, she mused, *but neither do happily-ever-afters*.

The chiming of her phone snapped her attention back to the present. She picked up the receiver. "Parrish here."

"Hi, Julie—Nathan here. I was wondering if you'd had lunch yet."

"Umm, as a matter of fact, no. I got lost in work this morning and forgot all about the time. I was just on my way out to get something."

"How about joining me for lunch in my office? I'll have something sent up and we can eat on the terrace."

"But it doesn't have golden arches," she said in mock protest.

"I can have the food served in little Styrofoam containers, if that will make you feel any better."

"Well, since you're so anxious to please—"

"What'll it be, Julie?"

She closed her eyes to think for a second. "Oh, fruit salad, I guess."

"I'll have the cafeteria send it up. Diet Seven-Up as usual?"

"You know me so well, I'll have to make some changes."

Nathan Bates laughed, and she thought he sounded almost boyish for an instant. She wondered quickly what he might have been like before he became one of the world's most powerful men.

"I'll be waiting for you," he said, and the boyish moment was gone. It sounded like a command.

"I'm on my way, boss."

As Bates hung up the phone, his other line rang. He put this one on intercom. "Yeah, Caroline, what is it?"

"McDougal from security, sir," said his assistant's voice from the speaker on his desk.

"I'll take it. McDougal, what's up?"

"Well, sir, we've managed to come up with some information on a weapons shipment heading for this area— from Central America, of all places."

"Why so surprised? We've sent so many guns down there over the years, they had to filter back sooner or later. You said you got *some* information. What does that mean?"

"It means we know it's coming, but we don't know exactly where or when."

"Then that doesn't do us a hell of a lot of good, does it?" Bates said testily.

"Uh, no, sir. I guess it doesn't."

The office door opened slightly and Julie came in. She saw she was interrupting and started to back out, but he motioned her to the chair opposite his desk and indicated the intercom.

"When you get me some useful information, you let me know. And it better be fast."

"Yes, sir," McDougal said.

Bates punched the intercom switch, then smiled at Julie. "Our lunches are on their way. Why don't we start with some wine on the terrace."

He stood, put an arm around her shoulders, and ushered her through the sliding glass doors to the redwood and concrete balcony overlooking the grounds of Science Frontiers. There was a telescope mounted on the railing. For Los Angeles, the air was relatively fresh. Bates poured some wine, but Julie shook her head.

"No wine for me—my blood sugar's so low from not eating, one glass'll go right to my head."

"Okay then, have a seat." He pulled out a white wrought-iron chair and they sat at the glass-topped table.

"This is the first time I've seen you since your meeting with Diana the other evening," Julie said. "How did it go?"

"Well, obviously I survived my encounter with our alien dragon lady. Not that it was particularly pleasant."

"What was so urgent that she absolutely had to see you?"

Bates took a sip of wine. "Well, you see, Diana doesn't have a fondness for being shot at or having her people blown up by the resistance. Seems she thinks weapons are being run in on some kind of underground pipeline to help your old resistance buddies right here in L.A. And we all know who's *supposed* to be in charge around these here parts, little lady," he said in a mock cowboy accent.

"You."

"Bull's-eye. Which incidentally is what Diana said she would turn L.A. into if I didn't put a stop to the gun-running under my jurisdiction. So the combined forces of Science Frontiers are being applied to breaking this gun-running pipeline as soon as humanly possible. If I don't succeed, Diana says she'll level the city, and she doesn't give a damn how much red dust we throw at them. She'll have her say, then just walk away from the ruins."

Julie bit her lower lip and her face telegraphed her

concern before she could cover it up. Bates saw it. *Damn*, she thought, *he notices everything!*

"I can understand you'd be worried about what might happen to some of your former colleagues. Yes, some of them could get killed. This is no game we're playing here. The survival of L.A. as a free and open city is at stake. And I don't plan on giving it up without a fight."

"But we're supposed to be fighting the *Visitors*, not each other, Nathan!"

"There doesn't have to be a fight, Julie. If you're still in touch with anyone you fought with in the resistance, I'd suggest telling them to forget the weapons shipment that's coming in. Oh, yes, we know a big shipment is due. And in very short order, we'll also know when and where it's due. We'll stop it—and if some people get killed, that's the way it goes." His dark eyes bore in on her. "Tell them, Julie. Tell them to give it up and lay off the Visitors in my territory."

She thought of looking away. In the pit of her stomach, she felt completely intimidated. But she wouldn't give in. "Nathan, you know they can't do that. They knew the risks when they decided to pick up the fight again. You do things your way because of who and what you are. Well, they're just doing the same thing, but their own way. That's how I would feel if I were still with them."

Bates smiled. "Which, of course, you're not. If they could pump your brain for the things you hear from me, I'd be in a lot of trouble. But I know I can trust you from top to bottom."

He patted her hand, and she felt like slithering away. But their lunches had arrived on a cart sent up from the company commissary, and they began to eat.

Donovan was pacing on a hillside above the city when he saw Julie's red Mazda climbing the road. She parked next to his Blazer and walked over to the stone wall bordering the overlook.

"How're you doing?" he asked.

She nodded and shrugged simultaneously.

"Are you sure about that?"

She managed to laugh, and they slowly, gently leaned into each other's arms. "It's nice to get a cuddle, Donovan."

"Yeah—nice to get one back. I wish we could do it more."

She looked up at him with a deep sigh. "I do too. But wishing's not everything."

Donovan raised an eyebrow. "That could be our epitaph, kid."

Julie pushed him back to arm's length. "My, we're sounding defeatist today."

"Sorry. It just gets hard to keep looking for silver linings when there's this many clouds around."

"Well, Michael, my love, I've got another cloud for you."

"Oh, no."

"Bates is onto the gun-running network."

Donovan swung away from her. "Goddamn him. What's it to him?"

"What do you mean, 'What's it to him?' " she asked incredulously. "You know damn well. He thinks this is his city and he thinks that what you do—what *we* do—is going to destroy it. Diana's lit a fire under him. She ordered him to stop the weapons shipments to us or she'll destroy L.A. herself."

"And she'll do it too. She's just crazy enough to do it out of spite," Donovan said angrily.

"Maybe we should cool it for a while. Lay low, conserve our resources."

He whirled to face her, eyes flashing. "Julie, we don't *have* any resources to conserve! That's the problem. Did you enjoy attacking that skyfighter with no extra ammunition? Well, I sure as hell didn't enjoy watching you do it, knowing . . ." His voice trailed off.

"Not forever, Mike—just for a while. We can hold our own."

"And what if we can't? What if Diana's got something planned that we don't know about? What if she pops a surprise attack somewhere important and we've got our fingers up our noses instead of on rifle triggers? We can't do it—*no way.*"

"Then we run the risk of Bates's tracking us down and putting us out of business for good."

"Can't you do something? You're such good buddies with the man. Talk him out of it."

"I can't talk him out of anything."

"Then do more than talk—do what you have to do. You want to anyway."

With a roundhouse swing, she slapped his face hard. The stinging blow knocked him off balance, and he rubbed his jaw.

"I'm sorry," Donovan said in a low voice. "I shouldn't have said that."

"No, you shouldn't have," she said in ice-tinged tones. She glared at him. She wanted to hit him again, pummel him for being so gaddamned crude and insensitive, but she'd settle for a verbal attack. "I walk a tightrope every day I go to work, Donovan. I go in there and work for that man, and he not only pays me well, he trusts me and confides in me. And even if I thought he was the worst bastard in the world, which I don't—right now you're creeping up in that category—even if I thought he was the worst, I'd still feel like I was betraying someone who trusted me. Do you know what that does to me every time I have to do this?" Her voice was shaking and so were her hands. She hated being so emotional and thought, *Why the hell can't I be a tough son of a bitch like these men?*

Donovan couldn't look her in the eye. "Yeah, I know, I'm sorry—I really am. I had no right to—"

"You sure as hell didn't."

"Look, we're not discussing this very intelligently, thanks to my big mouth. We should talk it over with the others tonight."

"Fine," she said, then turned, got into her car, and drove off without looking back.

Donovan's shoulders slumped as he watched her go. He'd wanted to say something but decided silence was better at this stage. "Donovan, you stupid ass," he mumbled to himself.

"No way," Ham Tyler said firmly. His manner made it clear that he wanted no arguments from the other resistance members gathered downstairs at Club Creole.

"That's what *I* said," Donovan added. "I haven't changed my mind."

"We need those weapons too badly," Tyler said, looking at Julie. "Without 'em we got nothin', and I don't want to face lizards with nothin'."

"Then we risk everything we've got," Julie said forcefully, addressing the group instead of Donovan or Tyler. "I know better than any of you how thorough Bates's people can be. If he wants something done, they get it done."

"But he's one of you," Elizabeth said quietly. She sat in a corner with Kyle Bates hovering protectively near. "Why would he do anything to hurt you?"

"Because Nathan Bates isn't one of anybody, honey," Donovan said softly, trying to avoid taking out his own frustration on the star child. "He answers only to himself, to his needs. We can't rely on him to help us, and we can't waste a lot of time and energy worrying about him either."

"If you don't worry about him," Julie countered, "you'll have more to worry about than you know what to do with."

"Okay, okay," Tyler said, raising his hand for quiet. "You've heard both sides of this argument—it's time to vote. Everybody got a piece of paper and something to write with? Okay, go to it. Elizabeth, collect 'em, please." He handed her a shoebox and she circulated around, picking up the ballots as people marked and folded them. As the proprietor, Elias counted them, then cleared his throat when he had the tally.

"Here goes, folks. Just remember, I only counted 'em, I didn't make 'em up. So if you're on the losing side, don't blame me."

"Let's have it," Ham said impatiently.

Donovan had sat stonefaced through the proceedings, and didn't alter his expression now as the results were readied.

He was unaccustomed to being on the same side of an argument as Ham Tyler, and he hated being at odds with Julie.

"Nine say forget the weapons shipment," Elias announced, "and fifteen say go get 'em." Elias listened to the group's audible release of breath, then dropped the ballots back into the box. "That's all, folks."

Donovan approached Julie. Her glare was still hostile. "Hey, I—"

She cut him off savagely. "I don't want to hear it, Donovan. You and Ham won fair and square, but I've got to point out that when I lead the group down to San Clemente to pick up this precious weapons shipment, we're the ones who're going to be front-line cannon fodder if Bates tries to intervene. Not only can we lose a lot of important people, but I could blow my cover with Science Frontiers, and then we lose an incredible intelligence supply. So you and Ham and the others better be right about this—or we're in a hell of a lot of trouble."

Chapter 6

The shift was half over. Barry had spent the past hours working in his own quarters for the sake of privacy, his computer channeled through Lydia's security lock. The more his research progressed, the more he realized Lydia's plan *could* succeed—and the more imperative it became to get word to the L.A. resistance.

His door chimed softly, and he reacted by reaching for a hand weapon and blanking out the computer screen. He wanted to take no chances until he could see who was calling on him. He pressed the release button and the door panel slid open. A younger officer stood in the hatchway, frizzy blond hair silhouetted against the backlight from the corridor. Barry's own cabin was nearly dark.

"Come in, Zachary."

The young officer entered and Barry closed the door behind him, then indicated a high-backed chair at the corner of the desk. Zachary sat down. "I left my post as soon as I could after I got your message, Captain. Why did you want to see me?"

"A mission of the greatest importance, Lieutenant. I'd do it myself, but I'm working on a special project for Lydia, and it would arouse her suspicion if I left the ship now."

Zachary leaned forward eagerly. "Left the ship, sir? For what?"

"You were recommended to me by your fifth-column cell leader."

Now Zachary sat back, tensing. "I'm sorry. I don't know what you're talking about."

"Yes, you do, Zachary. I'm the fifth-column leader in the security division."

The younger officer let out a low whistle. "There's fifth-column activity right under Lydia's nose?"

"Everywhere, Lieutenant," Barry said with a nod. "Are you willing to try something of grave importance and grave danger to yourself?"

"I could be an idiot and say yes without knowing what I'm getting myself into, or I could say, 'Tell me what the mission is and then ask me again.'"

Barry smiled. "If you hadn't said the second part, I wouldn't have believed you." As Zach listened closely, he explained Lydia's attack plan and the power-grid vulnerabilities he'd been studying in preparing the special report. "My report will be ready for Lydia by midmorning Los Angeles time. It's the middle of the night down there now. I need you to go there, make contact with Mike Donovan, and warn them about Lydia's plan—and tell them I'll get a copy to them as soon as I'm done with it."

"If they know what's coming, they might be able to stop it?"

Barry nodded. "That's what I'm counting on. Will you do it? I asked you because I know you have unlimited access to the skyfighters."

"That's what I get for being an engineering and repair technician—invited to fly down to Earth and risk my life in the middle of the night," Zachary said ironically. "Of course I'll do it!"

"Good. Let me tell you where you have to go, and bring Earth clothing with you. This has to be undercover." Barry activated the computer again and punched up a map of Los Angeles. He narrowed the view to the neighborhood around Club Creole and pointed out the alleyway where Zachary would find the entrance to the resistance hideaway.

"Are you serious? They really have a place like that right in the middle of this supposedly demilitarized city?"

"And what do you think *we've* got in Diana's little

legation, also right in the middle of the city?" Barry said with a snort. "Demilitarized is a relative term, Lieutenant. You'd better be leaving now—and be careful. Remember to report to me as soon as you get back to the ship."

The skyfighter set down in a small park a half mile or so from Club Creole. Dressed in jeans and a windbreaker, Zachary jumped out the hatch and watched as the pilot, another fifth columnist, lifted off. Zach turned and tried to get his bearings in the dark city, then decided he'd better consult the map Barry had charted for him. He took a palm-sized holo-reader out of a zippered pocket and thumbed the switch. The tiny screen lit up with a street grid, and Zach figured out the correct direction. He left the park, crossed a street, and made the first right turn.

He went straight for several blocks, then made a left and a right and found himself on a narrow street with its overhead lamps out. He squinted into the darkness, searching for the alley, nearly tripping over garbage cans hiding in shadows like hunkered-down animals. He winced at the clattering noise, set a can upright—and was promptly grabbed from behind by a pair of very strong arms. They closed around his chest and throat, and someone else slugged him across the back of the head.

When Zach regained consciousness, his eyes throbbed and his throat was parched. His hands and feet were tightly bound. As he glanced about, he saw he was in a dim, windowless room. From his vantage point, lying on his side on a cot, he seemed to be alone. *This must be the secret headquarters under Club Creole,* he thought. Then he felt a bulky human presence looming behind him, and turned his head to look.

"Who the hell are you, and why are you out of uniform?" Chris said quietly, arms crossed over his barrel chest.

Zachary swallowed, trying to raise some moisture in his mouth. "I—I'm with the fifth column. Barry sent me to see Donovan. It's very important."

Donovan stepped into the room and stood next to Chris. "I'm Donovan."

"Do you always treat your allies like this, Mr. Donovan?"

"No, but when we spot someone lurking around what's supposed to be a secret entryway, we don't take any chances. We prefer to have advance warning when guests are going to arrive."

"I—I can understand that," Zachary said, hoping they would notice how uncomfortable he was. If they did, they weren't doing anything about it. "Could you untie me, please?"

"No, we can't," Chris said, not unkindly.

"Not until we hear what you have to say," Donovan added.

"Oh. Well, could I sit up at least?"

"I guess so," Donovan said. He and Chris propped the visitor up against the wall and stretched his legs out. "How's that?"

"Better. Now, this is what's been happening. Barry has been working on some sort of special project for Lydia. It's something to get back at you for taking her prized prisoners, and something to clean her tarnished image with Diana— maybe grab a little extra power at the same time."

Donovan swung a wooden chair over and sat down. "Sounds serious. What are the details?"

"Well, it's an invasion plan, but I don't know anything about it. Barry's report to Lydia on its feasibility is due in a few hours. He's been working all night on it. As soon as he delivers the report to Lydia, he also wants to deliver a copy to you so you know what to expect."

"When's he gonna deliver it to us?" Chris asked.

"By ten o'clock in the morning, your time."

"Dammit," Donovan said. "We'll be long gone by then."

Zachary tilted his head. "Gone? Where?"

"We're getting one of the freed spies out of the country."

"This sounds pretty important, Mike," Chris said. "Maybe we oughta switch things around."

"We can't. But you're right—we've gotta see this report as soon as Barry can get it to us. The only thing we can do is rendezvous en route. Barry can meet us the same place and time as we're meeting Art Grant and handing over Maragato. What's your name?" he asked the trussed-up Visitor.

"Zachary."

"Okay, Zach. You tell Barry we want that report, but he's going to have to get it to us while we're traveling."

"Just give me the coordinates where I can find you."

A storage room down a narrow hallway from the speakeasy's main chamber had been converted into a sleeping area, and Kyoshi Maragato lay on his cot, eyes open. He was breathing steadily and evenly. He saw a shadow in the doorway and addressed it without moving. "Something troubles you, Mr. Tyler?"

"What makes you think so?" Ham parried.

"I sense it."

"Why aren't you sleeping?"

Maragato sat up. "I was meditating. It's my habit at this time each night. You are interrupting."

"Life's tough all over, isn't it?"

Maragato cocked his head at Tyler, who still hadn't budged from his position leaning on the door frame. "Is there something you wanted to discuss with me? Because if there isn't, I'd prefer to be left alone."

"You ever been to Korea, Maragato?"

"Yes, I have. As an intelligence agent, you're certainly aware that Japan has extensive dealings with the Korean CIA."

"I've worked the territory myself," Tyler said. "In fact, I'm surprised we never crossed paths."

"Our paths have crossed now, though. I'm grateful to you and your group for engineering my forced release from the Visitors. We Japanese believe in karma, Mr. Tyler— fate. Do you?"

Ham shook his head. "Nope. Nobody makes my life go in any direction I don't want it to go. Fate is bullshit. No offense."

"None taken—we all have our own beliefs."

"Maybe we do and maybe we don't."

"Are you saying you have *no* beliefs?" Maragato asked, polite surprise in his tone.

"I believe in me," Ham answered simply.

"You have a formidable reputation in the intelligence field. Perhaps that belief is well-founded."

"I don't put much stock in what other people think of me, Mr. Maragato. Doesn't sway me one way or the other."

"But your life is intertwined with the lives of others, isn't it? Do you truthfully believe your fates aren't commingled, perhaps in ways not entirely under your control?"

"I tell other people what to do, not vice versa. They know I go my way. I'd do it with 'em or without 'em. And I assure you I'd wind up in the same place either way."

"The belief in karma encompasses that. Whether you believe it or not, it is there."

"You sure we've never met before, Maragato? I swear I've had this conversation with you before."

Maragato smiled in the darkness and his white teeth flashed. "Maybe you just remember watching *Shogun* on TV, Mr. Tyler. Good night." He stretched out on his back.

Ham couldn't see if Maragato's eyes were open or closed. He stayed in the doorway for a couple of moments, then turned and left, heading for the main room for a drink before he tried to catch a quick few hours of sleep. Maybe Chris was right about Maragato. Maybe they *should've* blown the Japanese agent away. There was definitely something off base about him. Why didn't he remember him? Tyler shrugged to himself. He had a strong feeling that there was going to be trouble tomorrow. *Maybe there is something to this karma stuff after all*, he thought, *but I wouldn't bet on it.*

Chapter 7

The phone next to Nathan Bates's bed rang urgently. The digital alarm clock told him it was 4:50 A.M., but he'd been awake for the last half hour. He reached for the phone.

"Bates."

"This is McDougal, sir. I think we've got it."

"I'm listening."

"We cracked a coded message. The shipment is coming in today. One P.M., south of San Clemente. One of two ships—we're tracking both just to be on the safe side."

"If there's any doubt, intercept both, and do it far enough from their destination that nobody's watching. And call me the second you've got those ships boarded."

"Yes, sir."

SAN CLEMENTE ISLAND, 4:55 A.M.

The island lay about seventy-five miles off the California coast, in the Outer Santa Barbara Channel, south of the recreation islands of Catalina and Channel Islands National Park. San Clemente Island had been the site of a U.S. military reservation, used for war games and exercises, with small stocks of weapons and vehicles kept there. Mostly, it was populated by goats. The south end of the island formed a natural harbor called Pyramid Cove, and it was there that part of Nathan Bates's private navy anchored. At the moment, the force consisted of four patrol boats and several smaller speedboats for reconnaissance. The patrol boats were armed, and as they set out to intercept the cargo ships containing weapons bound for the resistance, the Bates crewmen were readying their own weapons. The four boats started their engines and sailed out of Pyramid Cove in line. Once in open water, they split into pairs and followed their scanners.

Ham, Donovan, Chris, and Kyoshi Maragato loaded small packs into Donovan's four-wheel drive. Sunrise tinted the cloud bottoms a blood red, though the sky was still a deep predawn blue everywhere but in the east.

The bald-headed, clean-shaven Japanese spy was now wearing a wig, mustache, beard, and glasses. "Are you sure all this was necessary?" he said to Donovan.

"Your own mother wouldn't recognize you, and if we run into any Visitors searching for their lost prize, let's hope they won't either." He climbed into the driver's seat and started the engine. "Let's hit the road."

Maragato and Chris climbed in the back and Tyler rode shotgun—literally. A Visitor laser rifle rested in his lap.

"What if these trail guides you know aren't there anymore when we get to Crow's Fork?" Donovan said, turning out of the garage onto the street.

"They'll be there."

Donovan glanced over at Tyler, who seemed preoccupied. "Something on your mind?"

Tyler continued gazing out the windshield. "Just your driving, Gooder. How 'bout keeping your eyes on the road? Wouldn't want you driving off a mountain, now would we?"

"No, I don't suppose we would."

"Where you headed?" Chris asked from the rear seat.

"Route Five—the back way."

Kyle glanced at the sun as it edged up over a bank of clouds. Then he stopped, gripped the garage door handle, and threw open the door. Julie drove the first small panel truck out, with Elias at the wheel of the second one, with Willie riding with him. When they were both out and idling in the driveway, Kyle swung the door down, took a last look at the nondescript warehouse, then vaulted up into the cab of Julie's truck. Elizabeth sat in the middle of the seat, plainly excited about being included in the pickup mission.

Julie flicked on her turn signal, then pulled out onto the street, making sure Elias' vehicle was visible in her side mirror. Both trucks had their headlights on in the early morning dimness.

"How long is the ride?" Elizabeth asked.

"Maybe an hour," Julie said. "Assuming there's no trouble. I hope Donovan and Tyler have smooth sailing."

"Are you and Donovan mad at each other?" Elizabeth asked.

Julie's eyes left the road for a second to look at the star child. "Yeah, I guess we are."

"I thought you loved each other."

"I thought so too," Julie said a little wistfully.

"But aren't you sure?"

"I don't know if you're ever really sure."

Elizabeth looked at Kyle for a fleeting moment, and Julie caught the look out of the corner of her eye.

"Why, what's on your mind, Elizabeth?" she asked.

"I'm—I'm just trying to figure out emotions and everything. I know my mother didn't love Brian, but they made love anyway."

"Your mom thought she loved Brian when she did that—and she thought he loved her. He lied to her. Besides, your mother was—is—still pretty young to have all this completely figured out."

"Are you old enough?" Elizabeth wanted to know.

Julie laughed. "Evidently not. How about you, Kyle? Got any contributions to make to this investigation?"

"You must be kidding. I don't think anybody's ever old enough to understand love."

Barry held the small tape cassette in the palm of his hand. In it was all the data Lydia would need to carry out her nighttime invasion. The idea had a mad genius to it, and, frankly, he'd been surprised, never thinking Lydia had the imagination to come up with something like this. He'd expect it from Diana, but not from his security commander. He'd thought of faking the report or suppressing the most vital facts and figures, but it was all there in the computer banks. He had the feeling that if his report didn't come up with the conclusions Lydia wanted to see, she would simply commission another aide to redo the research. She seemed *that* convinced of the rightness of her strategy.

He inserted the cassette into his terminal, then slid a blank one into a second slot. He touched the keyboard and watched as a copy was made within seconds. Then he reached for the intercom.

Zachary was trying unsuccessfully to rest when his own intercom chimed. "This is Zachary."

"This is Barry. Report to my quarters, please."

Zachary rolled off his bunk and slipped his boots on. "On my way, Captain."

The young officer hurried out and strode down the corridor. When Barry's door slid open to let him enter, he found the older officer playing a triangular stringed instrument. Zach sat down.

"I didn't know you play the *ta'iyta*."

Barry laughed. "Lately, I'd forgotten myself. I brought this little one with me hoping I'd keep in practice, but I can't recall the last time I had a chance to take it out."

"It sounds nice, sir."

"Thank you. You know, it took me years to master the fourteen-string version. I'd learned the seven-string when I was young, but like most children, I hated to practice. My father said it would teach me discipline."

"That's probably what made you hate it," Zachary joked.

"You're probably right. At home, I have four antique *ta'iytas*. They're handmade—worth thousands if I ever wanted to sell them."

"Do you?"

Barry shook his head. "No, I want to go home and play them." He leaned back in his chair and closed his eyes. "I want to play music, I want to strip off this human casing, I want to sleep late and write poetry in the evening on my veranda, I want to swim in the Lantan Hot Springs and lie out on a rock, just warming in the sun." He paused, took a mournful breath, then opened his eyes. "I don't want to fight this battle anymore."

Zach was quiet for a moment. "Is that the report?" he asked gently, pointing to the cassettes—three of them—on Barry's desk.

"Yes."

"When do you want me to take it to the resistance?"

"I'm going to go myself."

"But you can't leave the ship without Lydia thinking—"

Barry raised his hand. "I've figured out a way to do it without making her suspicious."

"Can't I go with you?"

"No, I want you here." Barry handed Zachary one of the cassettes. "Take this. Hide it. Don't look at it, don't mention it to anyone. You will have one of the three copies of this damned report. I'm taking one with me to give to Donovan, and I'm giving one to Lydia. If anything happens to me and I don't get this copy to the resistance, you'll be the only one standing in the way of Lydia's succeeding with her crazy plan for invasion. I'll leave it to you to figure out a way to get it to Donovan and the others. But you have to be patient—don't jump into things at the first sign of trouble. You'll have to use good judgment and confirm that I failed in my mission. Understood?"

Zachary nodded. "Yes, Captain."

Zachary left and Barry took the report to Lydia's quarters. Her satisfaction was obvious as she held the cassette like a treasure. "I'm sure your work is as thorough as usual, Captain."

"There's something I wanted to add to the report, but it would've taken more time than I had."

"Was it important?"

"I think so, Lydia. But I'd have to leave the ship and do some inspections of certain sites on Earth."

"How long do you think it would take?" she asked.

"Oh, a few hours, maybe half a day at most. With your permission, I'll leave right away. That way, you can review what I've given you, and then you'll be ready to see the addendum later on."

The security commander nodded. "That makes sense, Barry. All right, get to it. I'll be waiting for your extra information."

"Thank you, Commander." He saluted and backed out of her cabin.

When the door had closed, James came around the partition separating the office area from Lydia's sleeping cubicle. He wore only a robe. "Well?"

Lydia answered with a sly smile. "I think everything is going according to plan. It appears that Barry is being very cooperative in delivering our invasion strategy to Donovan and the resistance. I would say our lure is doing its job."

"And with our dual trap, it's very unlikely that Donovan will get away this time," James said, coming to Lydia and massaging her neck. "Are you going to destroy that report cassette?"

"No, I think I'll take a look at it. Before he became a fifth-column traitor, Barry was quite good at strategic planning. He's so concerned about keeping up his cover, he's probably done an excellent research job. Maybe we might yet get to use this invasion idea—when I'm supreme commander."

He leaned over to kiss her. Their tongues snaked together until she pulled away. "Did you make sure Barry's skyfighter has a homing beam?"

"I assigned someone to—"

She spun on him angrily. "When I give you an order, you don't delegate it. You see to it yourself. Now get dressed and get down to the hangar deck. Hurry up—he'll be leaving any minute."

He ducked his face to avoid Lydia's glare. "Yes, Lydia. Right away."

James watched from the control room high above the hangar deck as Barry climbed up into the cabin of one of the small skyfighters. A young technician trotted up as the hatch was about to close and Barry leaned down to talk to him.

James looked down at his tracking console, tapped the keyboard to enter the identification number of that particular vessel, and nodded to himself when the readout screen flashed to indicate the homing signal was strong and clear.

"What is it?" Barry asked in a low voice.

Zachary handed the older officer a pocket-sized keypad. "I hooked this up to the ship's homing system. I don't trust Lydia, and I thought you might not want them to track you. Once you're about a mile from the Mother Ship, punch the buttons on this and it'll override the tracking signal. You'll be out of visual range by then, and they'll lose you for sure."

"Thanks, Zachary," Barry said. "I don't have any reason to think Lydia suspects anything, but you're right—better to have some insurance."

Zachary patted him on the shoulder and Barry disappeared into the small spacecraft. With a mechanical whirr, the ladder retracted and the hatch closed. As he stepped back, Zach watched the skyfighter lift off the deck and edge toward the giant hangar bay opening. When the force-field signal showed clear, the vehicle accelerated through and banked away from the Mother Ship, heading toward the planet's surface a mile below.

Chapter 8

"You lost the signal?" Lydia whispered, voice chilled with incredulous fury. She rose to her feet and stood face to face inches away from James. "How could you lose the signal?"

"I—I don't know, Lydia. I personally checked it before he left the hangar deck."

"And was it working?"

He looked annoyed at her condescension. "Of course it was working."

"Well, it isn't now. If this is the kind of performance I get from my handpicked aides—"

"Lydia," he implored, "it wasn't my fault. How could it be my fault if he somehow figured out that you were using him?"

She glared at him dangerously. "Watch your step, James. Aides and lovers are not irreplaceable when they cross the line of insubordination. He could not have figured out that I was using him. It could just have been a precaution on his part. He may not yet know for certain that we're onto his little fifth-column scheme. In which case, our mission will still succeed, thanks to my planning a backup method of trapping Donovan. Let this be a lesson to you. If you're lucky, you'll survive long enough to make use of it someday. If you'd planned with necessary redundancies in mind, we wouldn't have had this little chat, and your career would not be in immediate danger."

* * *

Julie turned into the marina and drove her panel truck into the waiting, open garage. Elias followed in the second truck. They climbed out and surveyed the rendezvous setting.

"I thought this was supposed to be a decent-sized cargo ship we were meeting," Elias said, hands on hips as he squinted into the late morning sunshine. "This marina ain't big enough to handle a boat carrying more than a couple of forty-four Magnums."

"The cargo ship's docking offshore," Julie explained. "We'll move the stuff in with launches. Some of us are going to have to go out in the motorboats."

"I'll do that," Kyle volunteered. "I've been around water and've handled boats since I was a little kid."

"How about you, Elias?" Julie asked.

"I'd rather have my water in a glass with some Scotch, but I'll go out with the kid."

"Good. I guess I'll take one out with a couple of the others," Julie said, glancing back at the half dozen resistance members waiting in the welcome shade provided by the garage.

Elizabeth tugged at Julie's arm.

"What is it, honey?" Julie asked.

"I—I need to talk to you," Elizabeth said softly.

"Okay. We've got time while we're waiting. What's up?"

"I mean alone."

Julie nodded. "Oh. Okay. Hey, guys, keep a lookout. Let me know when our ship comes in," she said with an impish smile. Elias chuckled at the intended joke as Kyle continued to watch the horizon.

"Julie, don't go out to the ship when it gets here," Elizabeth said firmly.

"What? Why not?"

The younger woman's shoulders sagged. "I—I don't know. I mean, I *know*, but I can't explain it. I just feel like you're going to be in terrible danger if you go. Like you're going to get hurt, or killed."

Julie could tell that Elizabeth was on the verge of tears. It had cost the girl a great deal to break through her shell of shyness to tell Julie of her secret fears and visions. "Tell me what you saw, Elizabeth."

"I'm afraid. I don't want to see it again," she whispered. "But I had to tell you about it."

Julie gave her a hug. "Well, I'm glad you did."

Elizabeth brightened. "Does that mean you won't go?"

"I may have to, honey. I am in charge, you know," Julie said lightly. But the stab at humor didn't work. Elizabeth's face clouded over again.

"That doesn't matter. You're the one who could get hurt."

"But if it's dangerous for me out there, won't it also be dangerous for someone who goes in my place?"

"I don't know—I only saw it for you."

"When you see these things, what's it like? Do you see actual images or scenes of what's going to happen?"

The girl's brow furrowed. "No, it's more like a feeling— like when someone's standing behind you. You don't actually see them but you know they're there. Has that ever happened to you?"

Julie nodded. "Mm-hmm. But I think when *you* see something, it's a lot more definite than a premonition."

"Then you believe me?"

"Of course I believe you."

"Then you won't go." It was a statement, not a question.

"I didn't say that. I'll think about what you told me. And if you see anything else, tell me, okay? *Maybe* I won't go."

Elizabeth rested her head on Julie's shoulder. "I don't want anything to happen to you, that's all."

Julie stroked the girl's blond hair. "I know. I wouldn't want anything to happen to either of us. It'll be okay. Don't worry."

A bit of a breeze had kicked up, ruffling the fronds of the palm trees lining the shore. Julie walked Elizabeth over to the stone seawall so they could have some quiet time without the others around. The cargo ship wasn't due for at least an hour.

Elizabeth closed her eyes and basked in the warm

sunlight, sitting on the wall with her legs dangling. Julie sat next to her and watched her. She wished she could know what Elizabeth had seen, what went on inside that uncharted mind. Physically, Elizabeth seemed to have stabilized at the equivalent of eighteen human years, but from casual observation, Julie saw that each day of Elizabeth's life, her mind powers were continuing to develop at an irregular but ever-growing rate. If she'd actually had time to learn, some of the things the star child might have been able to do would have been remarkable. But in her topsy-turvy eighteen months of life, she'd barely had time to survive, much less be a student. That made her innate abilities nothing short of miraculous. Simply by touch, she could both draw data directly from computer banks and control them, as she'd done with the power reactors on the Mother Ships. She'd also demonstrated knowledge of ancient Visitor healing arts, again through touch, knowledge that dated back thousands of years, according to Willie. And only lately she'd begun to foresee future events. Her visions were blurred, skewed, light glimpsed through a prism. Julie could look at the girl's face and almost see her turning the prism over and over in her mind, trying to unbend the splintering light and make it come together in a reflection that made sense.

Julie wished she could help, for Elizabeth's peace of mind and for that of all of them. As the genetically engineered offspring of human and Visitor parents, no one knew what Elizabeth was becoming, what directions her powers would take. Not only was she a child in a young woman's body, she was also a wholly new and unpredictable life form.

And although Julie prayed against it, she knew that unpredictability in a world where Visitor armies stalked could spawn danger.

In the time since Donovan, Tyler, Chris, and Maragato had left the urban sprawl of Los Angeles behind, the sun had crept up from the horizon to its midday peak. The early part of the trip had been through the green hills of the mountain parks north of the city, but then they'd traversed the dry-dirt desert that makes up the spine of the state. The drone of the Blazer's tires combined with the heat and monotonous scenery to occasionally make Donovan drowsy. There hadn't even been a stray Visitor patrol to break the monotony. *Not a lot of chitchat either with this crew,* Donovan thought. Ham seemed even more caustic than usual, for reasons Donovan didn't want to begin to fathom.

About forty miles into the desert, Chris had made a stab at lightening the mood with a round of raunchy jokes, but Ham had been obviously uninterested and Maragato had been politely Oriental, while Donovan found it impossible to truly get into the spirit as a one-man audience. A shame since some of the jokes weren't half bad. He'd have to remember some of them and retell them to Julie—if they ever got back on speaking terms.

Donovan rubbed his eyes beneath his sunglasses and wiped an annoying bead of grimy sweat off his forehead. "I think I see a gas station up ahead," he said to no one in particular.

"Yep," Chris replied.

"Don't drive too fast, Donovan," Ham said. "That gas station means we're entering greater downtown Crow's Fork."

Donovan glanced around at the horizon. The sandy foothills had indeed become forest-covered mountains, but the change had been so gradual that he hadn't taken notice as Crow's Fork began to materialize up ahead.

The four-wheel drive slowed as Donovan lifted his foot off the gas pedal. The town was a dusty collection of one- and two-story buildings, looking like a western movie set, circa turn of the century. It had a partially paved main street, with dirt and gravel side roads branching off into the tinder-dry woods beyond. The few sidewalks were raised, some made of board, others of rough concrete.

"You're kidding about this, right?" Donovan said. "This looks like a ghost town. I expect to see Wyatt Earp at the O-K Corral."

"He moved out a few weeks ago," Ham said. "Not enough nightlife for the old guy."

"Where do we find your trail guides, Tyler?"

Ham pointed through the windshield. "Try heading over to the sign that says 'Trail Guides,'" he said dryly.

The sign really did read 'Trail Guides,' with the name O'Toole in front, and it hung over the doorway of a rough-hewn little house with a dormered roof and a raised wooden porch out front. Donovan stopped in a puff of dust, which hung in the still air and made his eyes itch as he swung open the truck door.

"Is O'Toole the guy you know?" he asked.

"I met him once when I came up here for a little recreation about two years ago. But Halsey's the name of the one I worked with in El Salvador. Damn good guide," Tyler said as he got out and moved the seat forward, letting Chris and Maragato squeeze out of the Blazer's rear compartment. Tyler led the way up the steps of O'Toole's place, knocked on the door, and pushed it open. A woman in her early thirties, her dirty blond hair in a bun, sat reading a magazine at a desk.

"Hey, Halsey," Ham barked.

The woman looked up reflexively, ready with a comeback before she was sure who'd spoken. She swallowed the words before she could say them and her blue eyes widened in disbelief.

"Whatsamatter, forget your name?" Ham prodded.

"Ham Tyler, you stinking son of a bitch," she snarled.

"Knows him well, huh?" Donovan said to Chris.

The big man shrugged. "Better'n you could ever guess, Donovan."

The woman's feral expression dissolved into a face-splitting grin, and she leaned across the desk. "Well, I'll be a son of a gun. What the friggin' hell are you doin' in Crow's Fork?"

"Came to see you," Ham said, standing in an unconcerned, arms-folded pose.

"The hell you did."

"Halsey, did your mother teach you to swear like that?"

She thought for a second. "First she taught my daddy, *then* she taught me." Slowly, as if thinking whether it was

worth it, she pushed her chair back and then ambled over to
Ham Tyler. As she did so, she revealed her slim, wiry
figure, clad in loose-fitting jeans and a denim shirt. Her face
had a sharp-featured, weathered beauty etched into it. For a
minute, Donovan wasn't sure if she was going to punch
Tyler or hug him. They hugged. Then she pushed him back,
her hands resting on his shoulders.

"Lemme look at you," she said. And she did—for an
instant. "On second thought . . ."

"Very funny, Halsey, very funny. Good thing for you my
ego doesn't bruise easily."

"Didn't know it bruised at all. Now, really, what the hell
are you doin' all the way up here?"

"We need your help. I knew you couldn't turn me
down—not after I saved your life in El Salvador."

"Hold on," she said ominously. "*I* saved *your* life."

Tyler scuffed the floor with his toe. "Oh, yeah . . ."

"You got the goddamnedest most selective memory I've
ever seen, Tyler. You know that?"

"Yeah," he growled. "You tell me that every time I see
you."

"Well, why the hell shouldn't I? You can't seem to
remember my phone number, but somehow you remember
me and find me every time you need a hand at somethin'
dangerous."

"I'm very selective who I ask on certain kinds of dates,"
he deadpanned.

"Okay, what's the date?"

"Just a local job," Tyler said. "You could do it with your
eyes closed. Nothing dangerous."

She narrowed her eyes at him. "Are you back in business
against the Visitors?"

"How'd you know about that?"

"I read papers, watch the tube. We got Cable News
Network up here, you know. You were a pretty big man on
campus after the so-called final battle. Wasn't too final, now
was it?"

"Nope," Tyler admitted. "And yeah, this has something
to do with the Visitors. Interested?"

"Hell, yeah," Halsey said. "Lizards're good for boots and that's about it. Be glad to help—for my usual fee."

"What ever happened to patriotism?" Tyler asked, shaking his head.

"Patriotism? I got paid in El Salvador—why shouldn't I get paid on my home turf?"

"I guess," Tyler said. "But I was CIA then. We don't have an unlimited petty-cash and dirty-tricks fund in the resistance."

"We'll settle the fee up later, Tyler. Maybe something private between you and me. What's the job?"

Tyler moved over and sat on the corner of her desk. "There's an old mine about two or three miles from here, up on the side of a mountain."

"I know the one," she said with a nod. "Fastest way up is by horse."

"Can you take us up there?" Donovan asked, finally able to break in on the conversation.

"Sure, no problem."

"How long will it take?" Donovan said.

"Oh, maybe an hour." She saw Donovan react with surprise. "Hey, if it was *easy* to get there, you wouldn't need me, would you?"

"I guess."

"Okay now, how 'bout telling me who these people are and why I'm taking you up to Skokie Mountain, Tyler."

"Fair enough. Mike Donovan, Chris Faber, Kyoshi Maragato, this is my good friend, Annie Halsey."

Donovan shook her hand, Chris nodded to her, and Maragato bowed in formal Japanese greeting.

"Mr. Maragato," Ham continued, "is an esteemed member of Japan's intelligence service. He and a couple of colleagues were captured by the Visitors. We *un*captured them. Now we're trying to get Mr. Maragato home to Japan, back to where he can do the most good fighting the lizards."

Annie nodded, a neutral expression on her face. "Sounds fine and dandy, Ham, but Skokie Mountain mine ain't Japan, the last time I looked."

He glared at her. "Mind if I finish?"

"Be my guest."

Donovan was having a hard time not laughing. He loved seeing Ham Tyler being verbally manhandled by a woman—or anybody, for that matter. It was fun sitting back and watching someone else do what he usually took upon himself.

"Fine," Tyler said testily. "I won't go into great detail. It's better for you if you don't know. But we're meeting some people up here who're going to take him and ship him home."

"And all you need me for is to take you there?"

Ham spread his hands. "That's it, Halsey. Simple?"

"Sounds simple," she answered suspiciously. "Though I can't say I'm thrilled about the part you said it's better my not knowin'."

Donovan stepped in. "Believe me, it is better. For you and for us. If things go wrong and the Visitors get their scaly hands on you, you won't have anything to tell them."

"Big deal," said Annie. "They'll probably still kill me just for the hell of it. You guys still get away 'cause I can't tell them what I don't know. Not so sure I like that. I'd rather have somethin' to bargain with."

"Not when it's our lives, honey," Tyler said sharply. "Now, do you want the job?"

"Sure, why not? But it's not entirely up to me. Hey, O'Toole!" she shouted toward a blanket-covered doorway.

The blanket moved aside, pushed by a meaty hand, and a big man with reddish-brown hair and a pale freckled face came in from the back room. He wore a plaid shirt with the sleeves ripped off, and fatigue pants.

"This is Frank O'Toole. He owns this place. Frank—Ham Tyler, Mike Donovan, Chris Faber, and Kyoshi Maragato." She filled him in on Tyler's request.

"Anything to do with Visitors makes me very, very leery, gentlemen," O'Toole said in a cultured accent bespeaking Ivy League schooling—an incongruous contrast to an appearance that smacked more of the Australian Outback then Harvard Yard. "Excuse me, I left a yogurt sitting back there. Anyone want one?" There were no takers, and O'Toole left the room to retrieve the white plastic container.

"Yogurt?" Ham whispered to Annie. "Is this guy for real?"

"Real men *do* eat yogurt," she hissed back.

O'Toole returned, spooning the yogurt into his mouth. "I suppose there's no reason not to take the job, but I don't want Annie going up alone. When's Alex coming back?"

"He just went to grab a beer at the general store," Annie said.

"All right, then, when Alex comes back, you and he can take these people up to the mine. And if he's not done with that beer, tell him to pour it down the sink. I want him sober for this trek."

Annie nodded, and O'Toole turned to the resistance members. "So, Ham Tyler returns. Well, I must say I heard a bit more about you from Annie here since your last visit. Quite an interesting career."

Ham started to crack a conceited smile and Annie noticed. "Yep," she said, "a bit more." She paused. "One or two things were even good."

Donovan and Chris smirked and Ham shot them a look. At that moment, the screened front door squeaked on its hinges and a rawboned man in his early thirties entered, dressed in an old Army shirt and jeans. He eyed the strangers and came over to kiss Annie quickly on the lips. "What's all this?"

"This is a job," O'Toole said. "Annie knows the specifics. I want you both to go."

"Guys, this is my boyfriend, Alex Kramer," she said, introducing him around the group.

Donovan took special care to note Ham's reaction to the word "boyfriend." There was none that he could discern.

"What time are you supposed to meet up with these folks?" Annie asked.

Donovan looked at his watch. "In just about an hour."

"If we're gonna make it, we'd better saddle up and get going."

Donovan held up a hand. "Uh, do you mind if we discuss something first?"

Annie shrugged. "Don't take all day. I'll go get the horses ready."

She left and Donovan motioned the others to one side.
"Not that we've got any reason to expect trouble, but I
think we should split up and take some precautions here."

"Split up? What do you mean, Gooder?" Tyler asked.

"I think you and I should go up with the guides, and
Chris and Mr. Maragato should wait back here. Don't
forget, we're also meeting Barry up at the mine. If Lydia
somehow follows him, I don't want Maragato caught in the
trap too. His safety is top priority right now."

Ham nodded. "Okay, makes a certain amount of sense.
Hell, once we've all gone up to the mountain, we've all
gotta come back down too. So we meet Grant's people and
Barry, then bring Grant back here and hand Maragato over
to him."

"Agreed, then?" Donovan said. Chris and Ham gave
their assent, and the Japanese agent had no objections.
Donovan turned to O'Toole, who was scraping the bottom
of the yogurt container. "Is that okay with you, Mr.
O'Toole—having two of our people wait here for us to come
back from the mine?"

"Sure, no problem at all, Mr. Donovan."

"Got your little friend with you?" Tyler asked Chris.

The younger man opened his fatigue jacket to reveal a
semi-automatic pistol tucked into its shoulder holster.
"Don't leave home without it."

Ham grinned. "Good. Hard to believe you were never a
boy scout." He checked his watch. "Donovan, are you sure
we've got time for this?"

"Yeah. Like you said, they have to come back this way
anyhow. We've got the time built into the schedule. They'll
have plenty of time to get back to Castillo Beach and meet
the sub off the coast."

"Okay then, we'll see you later," Chris said.

Annie Halsey poked her head into the main room from
the front doorway. "Ready to go?"

Ham turned. "Just two of us going with you—me and
Donovan."

"Hell. You made me get two extra horses ready for
nothing?"

"I'll make it up to you."

She gave Tyler a short laugh. "I doubt it, honey. Hey, O'Toole, you still want me and Alex to go?"

The Irishman nodded. "Better safe, etcetera."

Alex led Donovan over to a dappled horse and checked the saddle. Annie did the same for Tyler.

"Gotta say I'm disappointed in you, Halsey," Tyler said quietly.

She tightened the girth cinch of the saddle. "Oh, you do, huh?"

He nodded. "Your boyfriend looks like a real wimp. I thought I'd broken you of that habit down in El Salvador."

Her eyes flashed, but she reined in her angry retort. "El Salvador was El Salvador, here is here. People can't have real relationships with someone like you, Ham. Alex and I have somethin' nice."

Ham managed a cruel impression of a smile, sarcasm obvious in the curl of his lip. "Nice? That the best you can say?"

"It'll do," she said, slapping the horse's rump, making it bolt and catching Ham by surprise. He nearly fell off before snatching up the reins and grabbing the saddle horn to steady himself.

Donovan sidled his horse over to Tyler. "What was that all about?"

"Old rodeo trick. Mind your own business, Donovan."

The Visitor skyfighter skimmed over the California mountaintops, sunlight glinting off its metal skin. Barry sat next to the pilot and kept an eye on the navigation computer.

"This terrain all looks the same," the pilot said. She glanced at the navicomp.

Barry pointed to a pulsing spot in the center of the topographical chart glowing on the screen. "We're almost there. Drop me off, then leave and wait for my signal. If there's any trouble, I don't want you to get caught in Lydia's web."

"Trouble?" the pilot asked. "Zach said the locator beam would be disabled."

"I know, I know. Maybe I'm becoming paranoid working so closely with Lydia and Diana, but I can never shake the feeling that one or the other of them is somehow always right behind us no matter what we do."

The pilot nodded. "I don't think there's anyone in the fifth column who hasn't felt that way."

The horses moved in a ragged line, Annie taking the lead as they picked their way up the rocky trail rutted by rain and years of use. Donovan rode second, with Ham behind him and Alex bringing up the rear. When they reached a level clearing with a shallow stream, Annie signaled a halt and dismounted.

"Let the horses have a drink."

The others followed her order. Donovan tried to do a deep knee bend but fell over midway, groaning as he stretched out on the ground. "Geez, trail riding's a literal pain in the ass."

Annie sat next to him. "Outa shape, huh, Donovan?"

"For this, yeah."

Ham ambled over to Alex, who was lifting his horse's rear left hoof and checking the shoe. The young guide flashed him a warning look.

"Hey, if you don't want the company, kid, I'll leave you to the horse's rear end," Ham said.

"Look, Tyler, this is a job. I don't plan on getting terribly friendly with you."

Ham narrowed his eyes, weighing whether this was a challenge worth taking up. "Kid, I've got no beef with you. You got one with me?"

Alex put the horse's foot down and stood. "I know about you and Annie. I also know you hurt her by disappearing out of her life."

"Annie? Hurt? She's as tough as saddle leather."

"That's what I mean, Tyler. You don't understand her, you don't give a damn, and I wish you weren't here. But you are, I've got my job to do, so let's just keep it simple and civil. You stay away from her, don't even talk to her, and we'll get along fine."

Ham bounced on his heels for a second. "I see what's on your mind."

"Oh, you do, huh?"

Ham nodded. "Sure thing, kid. Annie's done some wild things in her life. She's seen more danger and excitement than you've ever read about. You know this backwater doesn't hold a candle to any of that, and neither do you. So I come back into the picture and you're scared shitless she's gonna realize that and run off with me."

"You're a conceited son of a bitch, Tyler."

"I'm also telling the truth. You don't much like that, do you, kid?"

"You call me 'kid' once more, it might be the last thing you say until your jaw heals," Alex said quietly.

"I'll think that over"—Tyler turned his back on the trail guide, then said over his shoulder, "—kid."

Alex clamped a grip on Tyler's arm. Tyler whirled, fist held high, and punched the younger man on the chin. Alex fell back and Ham leaped, but the guide rolled and Ham landed in the dirt. The advantage was lost and they grappled evenly. Donovan and Annie rushed over to separate them. Somewhere in the dust cloud rising from the battle scene, Donovan locked an arm around Ham's throat and hauled him out of the fray, leaving Annie to grab Alex and prevent him from giving chase.

"What the hell is this, a schoolyard?" Annie growled. "You two idiots don't have enough to keep you occupied on this ride?" She had a firm half nelson on her boyfriend and yanked him over to sit on a boulder.

Donovan loosened his headlock on Tyler. "If I let go, will you refrain from acting like an asshole?"

"Sure. I made my point," Ham croaked.

Donovan let him go. They faced each other as Ham smoothed his clothing and hair. "What point?" Donovan asked angrily.

Ham waved the question off. "You wouldn't understand, Gooder. You're into these newfangled open and equal relationships."

"Whereas you prefer the old tried and true Neanderthal

methods." Donovan smirked. "I'm not sure if this is good or bad, but you're not as one-dimensional as I thought, Tyler. As least one and a half, I'd say. It's interesting to see this other, romantic side of you."

"Hey, this has nothing to do with romance!" Ham flared.

"Why quibble over words? But we really don't have time for rutting season now, so keep it under wraps, huh?"

Annie brought Alex back over, shaking her head as she looked from one to the other. "I had a feeling I should've put choke collars on both of you. Do anything like this again, I'll push you both off the nearest cliff. Let's go—we've got distance to cover."

As they moved to the horses, Donovan leaned close to Tyler. "Try candy and flowers sometime, Ham."

Predictably, Ham swung, and Donovan ducked.

The skyfighter circled over the side of Skokie Mountain until Barry spotted a clearing about a quarter of a mile below the abandoned mine where he'd agreed to meet Donovan. The pilot dipped the nose of the sleek vessel and gently set it down, its directional thrusters kicking up puffs of dust. The gull-wing hatch lifted and Barry ducked under it and hopped down to the ground.

"This shouldn't take long once Donovan arrives, but I'm not sure how long I may have to wait," Barry said.

"I'll find some secluded place not too far away," the pilot said. "That way, it won't take me long to get back and pick you up in case any emergencies arise."

Barry nodded, tapped the hull, and backed away from the ship as the hatch drew down with a vacuum hiss. The antigrav engines whispered their farewell and the skyfighter drifted up, hovering for a moment and then accelerating away. It dipped around the mountain and was gone from Barry's sight. He took a small holo-reader out of his utility pocket and tapped in the code to call up the map Donovan had given to help him find the exact location of the mine. On the device's tiny screen, coordinate numbers appeared sequentially, along with a directional indicator. Barry glanced around, then started the rest of the way up.

* * *

After the fight, Donovan and Annie switched the order of those in the caravan, placing Alex in the lead and Ham at the rear. The remainder of the climb was uneventful, and they made good time. Donovan had always been amazed at the surefootedness of horses. Even as a kid, he'd loved to ride, knowing he could watch the scenery while the horse watched its own footing. Some horse people had warned him that he was giving the animals too much credit, but none had ever let him down. The dappled gelding he now rode was just as trustworthy as his past horses.

The warm midday sun was tempered by a cooling breeze, and Donovan leaned back in the saddle, letting sunlight fall on his face as rays speckled through the canopy of leaves. The rolling rhythm of the horse's walk lulled him near sleep.

"Don't get too relaxed," Annie said from behind him. "We're just about there."

"How far?" Donovan asked.

Annie pointed ahead. "Just around that corner there's a rise. The mine's just over that. Maybe ten minutes."

It took less. The mine wasn't much, just a tumbledown shack, with planks of wood rotting to gray splinters and a skeletal wooden overhang attached to the cave that led into the mountain.

"Anybody ever get anything out of this?" Ham asked while they surveyed the mine entry from cover of the trees.

"Yeah, the Skokie family did okay," Annie said, standing in her stirrups. "But that was, oh, sixty years ago. Place's been pretty much shut up for half a century, except when some fool prospector thinks he's gonna find a fortune in tapped-out veins, goes in, causes a cave-in and the police have to come and dig him out."

"How often does that happen?" Donovan asked.

"Oh, about once every few years. People just don't like to take no for an answer." She gestured ahead and Alex kicked his horse, leading them out of the woods into a tiny clearing overgrown by scrubby bushes. A stocky figure stepped out of the shadows of the mine entry and the horses skittered nervously. The red uniform shouted against the subdued greens and grays and browns of the mountain and old mine. Barry shaded his eyes as he came into the open and waited.

The mounted quartet crossed the sandy clearing and got off their horses. Barry came over to greet Donovan and Tyler.

"Were you waiting long?" Donovan asked.

"No—maybe thirty minutes. Well, I know you're in a hurry, and I'd better not waste time. Lydia thinks I'm checking out some important strategic power facilities to see if her insane invasion plan can actually be implemented."

"Your friend Zachary said it was an invasion plan, but he didn't tell us any specifics," Tyler probed.

"That's why I'm here," Barry said. He reached into his pocket and took out the holo-reader and one of the small information cassettes, than handed them to Donovan. "This is my report—I want you both to see it now, in case you have any questions. It's complicated, so we may not have much time to stop Lydia if she decides to go through with this."

"I thought you always said Lydia was more stable than Diana," Donovan snapped. "What the hell is she doing cooking up invasions?"

The Visitor shrugged. "Lydia's been under a lot of pressure—a lot of it added by your removal of her important prisoners. No, Diana was not at all pleased about that."

"Gee, we're sorry," Tyler said sarcastically. "Tell them both to get the hell off our planet and we won't put any more pressure on the poor ladies. We wouldn't want them to get gray hairs over us troublesome humans. Oops, I forgot, you lizards don't have hair, do you?"

"All right, let's get down to business here," Donovan said, leading Ham and Barry to some large rocks in the mine's entrance. They sat down and Donovan slipped the cassette into the reader device.

Chapter 9

"Willie, I need your opinion," Julie said quietly. She took the Visitor by the arm and guided him away from the rest of the group still awaiting the arrival of the cargo ship. The marina was deserted except for the resistance team, and Kyle and Elias continued taking turns with the binoculars, scanning the Pacific horizon for any signs of the weapons shipment.

"About what, Julie?"

She looked into Willie's eyes, and it occurred to her, not for the first time, that this being from a world almost nine light-years from Earth was probably the most trustworthy creature she'd ever met. He could always be counted on to answer any questions honestly, no matter what the consequences, and his loyalty was unswerving. So was his affection for the humans who'd taken him in and treated him as one of the family. "It's about Elizabeth—about her ability to see the future."

"Ahh," he said, nodding gravely. "You want to know if her ability is reliable or just a—a splash in the pan?" He looked triumphant, believing he'd mastered another colloquialism.

Julie smiled gently. It was so hard to correct him, knowing how hurt he would look. "That's flash in the pan, Willie."

His shoulders slumped.

"But you were very close," Julie added encouragingly.

"It doesn't matter," he sighed. "You did not take me

85

aside to give me a linguistics lesson. What concerns you about Elizabeth?"

"Is it common for your people to have the mental powers she seems to have?"

Willie thought for a moment. "Common? No. But it's not impossible. We've already seen that she knows things our Masters of the *Preta-na-ma* religion knew long ago. She's somehow learned these things by herself, since no one could have taught her."

"Or maybe she was born knowing them."

"How could that be?"

"We don't really know how much of Elizabeth's conception was natural and how much of it was controlled by Diana. Once she engineered the fertilization and implant of the embryo in Robin, she may have somehow conditioned Elizabeth prenatally."

"How?" Willie's face reflected a mixture of revulsion and curiosity.

"Well—" Julie searched for a way to explain it that would make sense to the alien, who had little medical training or knowledge of biology. "I haven't had any direct experience myself, but I've read about theories and even experiments on pregnant women and their fetuses. They're exposed to outside stimuli to see if unborn children are aware of their environment."

"Are they?"

"The research is really just beginning, so it's hard to say. But your science is advanced enough beyond ours that Diana may know of definite ways to influence the fetus at a very early stage. And don't forget she had Elizabeth with her for a while after she was born."

Willie was clearly troubled. "That seems wrong, to make a child anything it was not supposed to be."

"You're worried about Elizabeth, aren't you?" Julie said, touching Willie's arm reassuringly.

He nodded. "She's had so many terrible things happen to her in her short life—the deck has been cracked against her."

With a half smile, Julie let that one pass. "I don't think

Diana would've done anything to hurt Elizabeth, anything that would turn out negative later on. I mean, she went to a lot of trouble to create a child that would be a cross between our species. I think she planned on this being some sort of grand experiment."

"But Diana isn't good, Julie. I fear she may have had some very twisted motives when she did these experiments."

Julie nodded. "Maybe. But I think we'd have seen some evidence of that by now. I really don't think Elizabeth is a time bomb. In fact, I think she's one of the few positive things Diana's done. That's why Diana wants her back so badly."

"I guess you're right."

"Back to what I was asking about—do you think she can really see the future?"

"It's very possible, Julie. Why? Has she told you something she thinks will happen?"

"Mm-hm. And I need to decide if her warnings are worth a change of plan."

They heard shouts from the dockside and turned to see Kyle waving. "Hey, they're out there!"

Julie squinted, then saw a ship coming toward them, appearing just around the spit of land that protected the harbor. Elizabeth ran up to her, nearly bowling her over. The girl's face was tear streaked.

"Julie, I saw it again. Please, *please don't go to the ship!*"

Julie held Elizabeth at arm's length for a moment, then drew her into a hug. "Okay, Elizabeth, I won't go. I don't know *how* you know, but you know something—and that's good enough for me.

"Elias, you're in charge," Julie said as she, Willie, and Elizabeth rejoined the rest of the resistance members preparing to sail out to the cargo vessel once it dropped anchor.

"Hey, man, thanks a heap," Elias said sarcastically. "What do I look like, Long John Silver?"

"Did he own a restaurant too?" Julie asked innocently.

"Very funny."

"Hey, Julie," Kyle called from one of the trucks. "The ship's calling us. They want to talk to the person in charge."

Julie and Elias turned in choreographic unison, then stopped in place.

"Hey, I thought you said I was in charge," Elias protested.

"On the high seas, Elias." She climbed up into the truck cab, and Kyle handed the transmitter microphone to her. "Rendezvous One, this is Rendezvous Two. We read you."

A crackle of static spat from the dashboard speaker. *Roger, we copy. We don't have a motor launch on board— hadda leave port in a hurry. Hope you don't mind the inconvenience of coming out to us."*

Julie glanced at Kyle and Elias, her mouth curled in annoyance. "Nope," she lied. "No problem at all. Have you dropped anchor?"

"Roger on that, Rendezvous Two. We're ready for you."

Julie put the mike back on its dashboard hook and climbed down from the truck. Kyle and Elias stood in front of her.

"Okay, gentlemen, it's your show now," she said.

They moved quickly to the dock, where Kyle had already made sure the fifteen-foot launch was ready. He climbed down first, holding the boat steady for Elias, who gingerly let his toe touch the aluminum floor of the boat, then only very reluctantly let go of the dock piling. He stood in the center of the launch, swaying unsteadily.

"I'm gettin' seasick already," he called out plaintively to anyone who would listen.

"Oh, you're a big baby," Julie shouted down at him.

"If you don't sit down, you're going to be a big *wet* baby," Kyle snapped, grabbing Elias' hand and yanking him down on the middle bench seat. "Hold on, man."

Elias made a sour face. "What's this 'hold on' stuff? Give me a little credit, man."

"Suit yourself," Kyle said. He reached around, started the engine, and accelerated quickly away from the dock.

The nose of the boat lifted out of the water, and Elias promptly toppled over backward.

Julie and the others couldn't help laughing as they watched Elias rolling around, clamping his hands onto the gunwales in a vain effort to regain his balance, and his dignity.

Kyle steered the launch to the cargo ship as it lay in the middle of the harbor, rolling gently with the waves lapping at its sides. The *Mary Beeme* had seen better days. Rusty patches showed through her dark blue paint and her hull was scarred and dented from a lifetime of run-ins with tugboats, barges, and docks. As Julie watched through binoculars, Elizabeth clinging to her side, she knew that this old freighter carried the means to carry on the resistance. *Funny,* she thought, *I spent my life going to school to learn to save lives and here I am anxiously waiting for guns and ammo to kill people with.*

She gave herself a mental shake. *No, they're not people, kiddo, and they'd sure as hell kill you and your friends, given half a chance.*

As she observed, the launch reached the *Mary Beeme* and Kyle tied up alongside. Elias stood, staggered, and the younger man helped him grasp the ladder hanging over the freighter's rail. The black man climbed slowly up her side like a squirrel on a trellis—a very cautious squirrel. Then Kyle went up, hopped over the railing, and he and Elias were met by two of *Mary Beeme*'s crew. They led the resistance fighters through a hatchway and then they were all gone from Julie's sight.

While Kyle kept his eyes on the two men bracketing him and Elias as they walked quickly through a corridor, Elias sneaked glances at the ship itself. She was a sorry old bucket, with paint peeling and the smell of dank, rotting wood throughout, tempered with a strong undercurrent of mildew. Her cabins leaked, no doubt about it, and no one had cared enough to caulk and seal her.

But the men didn't look as if they matched old *Mary Beeme*. They didn't look like merchant seamen—their hair was too neatly combed, blue jeans and work shirts too new with no grease spots or sweat stains, faces clean shaven, not stubbly like those of sailors who'd been steaming up in a hurry from Central America for the past few days and nights.

Silently, Kyle and Elias each hoped the other noticed the things he was seeing, wished they could talk and compare notes, and hoped like hell they weren't walking into some sort of trap. The sailors weren't Visitors—they didn't have the reverberating voices the aliens couldn't really hide—but *who were they?*

The answer came when they went up a ladder, through another narrow passageway, and emerged on the bridge. There was a single man waiting in the control room. His back was to them, and he wore a red windbreaker emblazoned with the logo of Science Frontiers.

Nathan Bates turned to face his son and Elias Taylor. Both of them stood still, unable to move or speak for several seconds. Kyle Bates found his voice first.

"You son of a bitch," he hissed.

The elder Bates managed a sardonic grin. "No way to talk to your father, Kyle."

"You bastard," the young man continued.

Bates interrupted him. "If you're going to go through the whole book of words you can't say on television, I'm going to have my assistants remove you." He glanced at the stocky Bates security guards, who remained posted at the door.

"Be cool, man," Elias said to his companion. "No trouble yet. Let the man tell us what he wants."

"I want you and the other resistance fighters to stop your sabotage and attacks against the Visitors and against my company in Los Angeles."

Elias leaned back and eased himself onto a stool near an instrument console. "As long as we're taking requests, how about 'Old Man River' played on water glasses at Club Creole every time you come in, hmmm?"

"I'm not joking, Mr. Taylor. I'm serious. And what's more important, *Diana* is deadly serious—serious enough to threaten to blow L.A. off the globe if something's not done to stop the hostilities under my jurisdiction."

"Your jurisdiction," Elias said, clucking his tongue. "That's what it's all about, isn't it, Bates? Your little kingdom's in the coals, man, and you're worried about it burnin' up."

Bates spread his hands, a gesture of admission. "You're a smart man, Mr. Taylor. Or can I call you Elias?"

"Sure, man, whatever you want." Elias jerked a thumb at the guards. "King Kong and Mighty Joe Young'll see to that, huh?"

"They won't touch you. They're just a—precaution, in case you'd decided not to be civilized while we discuss our mutual predicament."

"There's nothing mutual about it," Kyle said sullenly.

"Oh, but there is, Kyle, there is. Always has been. You and your friends haven't ever realized that, which is really a shame, because we're all on the same side."

Kyle allowed himself an incredulous laugh. "You're full of crap—*Dad*." The last word was sarcastic.

Bates settled into the captain's swivel chair and folded his arms. Kyle cut him off just as he was about to speak.

"Oh, we're about to get lectured by the great Nathan Bates, Elias. I saw that pose at least twice a week the whole time I was growing up."

"Obviously, it didn't have any effect on you, Kyle," Bates said. "Let's see if Elias has any more sense than you. It's really very simple. My deal with Diana was to accomplish one thing and one thing alone—stop the war here before there was nothing left. With Science Frontiers' people and resources, we'll find a way to beat the Visitors once and for all. But we can't do that if we've already been blown to kingdom come."

Elias folded his own arms to mirror Bates's posture. "And if along the way you get even richer and more powerful than you were before, that's no skin off anyone's nose, right?"

"I notice you weren't above finding a little personal gain

in your own fame after the first Visitor invasion," Bates said with a smile.

Elias returned the smile. "What I got I earned—*after* the war, in peacetime, without using anybody else as pawns in my own power game. If we don't do what you want, agree right here and now, are me and Kyle gonna disappear just like all your other enemies?"

Bates laughed mirthlessly. "Starting to believe your own propaganda, eh, Mr. Taylor? Bates the demon? Bates the traitor? Well, whether you care to admit it or not, I am on your side. We want the same things—peace, safety, getting rid of the Visitors. To prove it, I'm going to let you go."

"Gee, thanks, Dad," Kyle said.

Bates ignored his son's comment. "Do things my way, we'll all win in the end. But keep up this underground rebellion and we'll all die. I can almost guarantee it. That would be a waste, wouldn't it? Go back to your restaurant, Elias. I like the place—I'd hate to see it reduced to radioactive cinders, wouldn't you?"

Bates nodded to the guards, who moved in to escort Elias and Kyle back to their boat. Elias stopped at the door.

"Oh, uh, Nat, I don't suppose we can still take the weapons shipment with us?"

Bates shook his head. "You're a cool customer, Elias. You could learn a thing or two from him, Kyle. You're still too excitable."

"Hey, man," Elias said, "one last thing."

"Sure."

"How'd you find out about this shipment? I mean, you don't have to give away any trade secrets or nothin'. But just to satisfy my own curiosity."

"If you mean did the Visitors tip me off—no. Don't underestimate the resources of Science Frontiers. We can do things Diana would never suspect. It's one of the reasons I can deal with her on an equal footing. She thinks she's toying with me, but I may be the one who's doing the toying. Consider *that* when you think about whether you want to play on my team. Oh, and Elias, sit down in the boat on the way back. You're going to be a valuable asset to me someday. I wouldn't want you to fall into the bay and drown."

Elias tipped a salute. "Thanks for the concern, man. You're beautiful, I love ya," he said, Hollywood style.

As the guards took them back down to the deck, Elias shook his head. "Some dude, your old man."

"Sounds like you admire him," Kyle said bitterly. "He's a bastard and a traitor."

"Whoa, kid, I didn't say I *admired* him. But he does have his act together. It's a wonder he didn't take over the world *before* the Visitors came."

"Don't think he didn't try."

The security men helped them over the side and held the ladder steady until they were back in the motorboat. Kyle pushed away from the landing platform, started the outboard engine, and looked back at Elias. "You sitting?"

Elias rolled his eyes. "What does it look like, man?" He *was* sitting, feet planted firmly on the boat's floor, hands holding the sides, elbows locked. "I am not just sitting, I am ready for a high-impact collision with the QE II."

"Good." Kyle gunned the motor, swung sharply away from the *Mary Beeme*, and watched as Elias toppled over onto his back again. "You're not cut out for this seafaring life, are you, Elias?"

The black man looked up from his place on the floor. "Just drive the damn boat."

When they arrived back at the marina a few minutes later, their faces revealed that something had gone terribly wrong. Julie and the others gathered around to hear the details. Elizabeth listened for a while, then turned pale and drifted off to sit by herself in one of the truck cabs. As Elias continued the story of Bates's surprise, Kyle went to look for her.

He leaned through the truck window. "Are you okay?"

She shrugged. "I guess."

He extended his hand, and after a moment, she took it in her own. They stayed that way for a long, silent moment. Julie quietly joined them.

"Elizabeth," she said, "you might have saved my life today. Thank you."

"What do you think my father would have done if you'd walked onto that ship instead of me and Elias?" Kyle asked.

With a deep breath, Julie opened her eyes wide. "Oh, I don't know. But I don't think he'd have let me go. In his eyes, I'd be a traitor to him personally. He trusts me, Kyle. I don't think he'd understand my betraying him. To him, that would be worse than betraying the planet."

"Yeah," Kyle agreed, "he does tend to see things in narrow terms."

Julie allowed her shoulders to slump. "And I'm not sure he'd be wrong, Kyle. I am betraying him. Every day I go to work and find out secrets from Science Frontiers, and then I take them and turn them over to people who are sworn to fight him and the Visitors."

"That's not betrayal," Elizabeth whispered.

Julie tried to smile, but the effort fell short. It hadn't been at all a good day. "I don't know what it is, honey. I just know we're being pushed, a lot of us, into things we don't like doing. And when it's all over, if we win, I wonder how much damage the scars are going to do to us. What are we going to be like?"

"We'll be okay," Kyle said. "Don't worry."

Julie added her hand to Kyle's and Elizabeth's and gave them both a squeeze. "Well, Elizabeth, I may never understand how you know what you know, but I sure am glad you do."

"Me too," Elizabeth said.

Julie and Kyle stepped away from the truck as the rest of their group came over, ready to head back to the city. "But, damn," Julie said, "we needed those weapons. Okay, everybody, let's head home—and I sure hope Donovan and Tyler are having a better day than we are."

Chapter 10

Art Grant peered through the windshield of his pickup truck, his barrel chest pressed up against the steering wheel. He scratched his white Ahab beard and glanced at the muscular young man seated beside him. The truck towed a two-horse trailer behind it.

"Almost time to park and switch to horseback," Grant growled. "What do you think, Ramón?"

"I think we should do it here."

Grant nodded, resignation evident in the downward set of his lips. "Yeah, I suppose. My ass just isn't too anxious to get up in that saddle. Horses used to be fun before hemorrhoids."

Ramón snickered, earning a dirty look from the older man. Grant wrestled the pickup over onto the road's grassy shoulder and the two men climbed out and went back to the trailer. Grant's eyes narrowed and he looked around.

"Something wrong, Art?" Ramón asked.

"Nah. Just thought I heard something rustling in the woods. What do you suppose, two or three miles' ride from here to the mine?"

"Yeah, man, no sweat."

"That's easy for you to say," Grant retorted as they unlatched the tailgate. The bearded man straightened suddenly. When Ramón started to speak, Grant held up a hand for silence and cocked an ear. *Something's out there,* he thought. After a moment, the sound became clear, as if shaking itself free of the other natural sounds of the woods.

It was an unnatural whisper that echoed and multiplied. Grant tilted his face up to the sky.

Ramón waited, then heard it too. He also looked up.

Four Visitor skyfighters arced across the blue haze in a purposeful formation.

"Do you think those things are headed for Crow's Fork?"

Ramón shrugged. "I think so, Art. What's it mean?"

"It means something's screwed up, it means we better say a prayer for Donovan and his people, and it means we're getting back into the truck and getting the hell out of here!"

Grant's short legs churned like a cartoon character's and he vaulted into the driver's seat. The engine was on and the truck rolled forward before the doors were even shut. Spinning tires sprayed a hail of gravel and sand as the truck swerved in a clumsy U-turn and headed back the way it came.

"C'mon, O'Toole, what the hell kind of Irishman doesn't have a good bottle of bourbon or whiskey or *somethin'* ," Chris moaned. He kicked back in the old wooden chair, and its base springs creaked under his weight. With two leaden thumps, his heels landed on the desk. Maragato sat in a rocker in the corner of O'Toole's front room, and O'Toole himself rested against the door frame.

"What can I tell you, my friend? I guess I'm not your typical Irishman. The best I can offer you is orange juice, carrot juice, apple juice, or low-fat milk."

Chris covered his face with his hands. "Lordy, I'm gonna die of thirst. How long do you think it'd take that apple juice to turn to hard cider?"

O'Toole ignored the question. "What about you, Mr. Maragato? Can I get you anything?"

Maragato shook his head and smiled softly. "No, thank you."

Chris uncovered his face. "You don't eat much, do you?" he said to the Japanese agent. "Come to think of it, I can't recall seeing you eat a bite since we got you away from Lydia. Not even at the going-away party for Durning and Coopersmith."

"Have you been observing me that closely?"

Chris was annoyed that the man's voice retained its unflagging neutrality. He determined that it was time to break his reserve down, and in a hurry. "As a matter of fact, yeah, I have been. Care to explain?"

"No, I don't, Mr. Faber. My appetite is a private matter."

Chris slipped his jacket open and unholstered the semi-automatic pistol, aiming it in Maragato's general direction. "How'd you like to reconsider that opinion?"

"See here, Mr. Faber!" O'Toole said sharply, starting to stride between the two others.

Chris tipped the gun barrel away from Maragato for a moment. O'Toole stopped and backed up to his previous position. "Good move, Mr. O'Toole. I'd stay out of this if I was you." The gun moved back to Maragato. "Now, Mr. Maragato, you were about to explain your strange eating habits."

The Japanese man was no longer smiling, but the gaze was still controlled, level, still lacking in emotion. "You Americans aren't very subtle, are you? That's always been your style. You want an explanation? Very well. I eat only vegetables and sushi, and the cuisine offered since I've been under your group's protection has frankly not appealed to me. In addition, under normal circumstances, I don't eat or drink very much. It's a discipline I taught myself as part of our profession—useful at times, wouldn't you agree?"

"Okay so far."

"Lastly, when under conditions of extreme stress, such as my recent capture by Lydia and subsequent liberation by your people, it's my habit to fast, almost totally abstaining from food. It's a means of purging and cleansing the body and spirit, something you beer-swigging, red-meat-consuming Americans would hardly understand. I simply drink water and can sustain myself that way for quite a number of days."

"It's *been* quite a number of days," Chris pointed out. "I'd guess your stomach should be growling for something a little more filling than water about now."

"Guess all you like."

"Thanks, Maragato, I'll do that. And if you feel like eating, you let us know and maybe we can catch something to your liking." Chris put the gun back under his jacket, meeting Maragato's icy glare for several moments. *Broke the shell a little, at least,* he thought. He didn't feel the need to compete in any staring contest, so Chris turned and joined O'Toole at the front windows.

"What was that all about?" O'Toole asked in a whisper.

"I got some suspicions about our Japanese friend. If they turn out to be true, you'll know."

"I don't have the slightest notion what you're talking about."

Chris gave a short laugh. "Let's hope things stay that way." His gaze strayed out the window, and then he did a fast double take. "Holy shit!"

"What?" O'Toole said, then looked outside himself.

On the main street of Crow's Fork, California, four Visitor skyfighters landed in clouds of dirt. Their hatches swung open and thirty armor-clad shock troopers clambered out to form a box formation, weapons aimed in all directions. As Chris and O'Toole watched through the curtains, Lydia finally climbed out of the lead space vessel and calmly surveyed the town.

Chris's hand went reflexively to his gun, though it occurred to him that one man with a pistol wasn't going to do a hell of a lot of good against a Visitor occupation force.

"What on earth are they doing here?" O'Toole demanded.

Maragato had joined them at the window. "Looking for me, perhaps?" He sounded unconcerned considering their situation.

Chris glared at him. "You better hope this stupid disguise works." He looked back out at the street and saw that Lydia and several of her troops were headed directly for O'Toole's establishment. "Dammit. You got a place to hide, O'Toole?"

The trail guide nodded. "Yes, of course. This way."

Maragato stood still and Chris reached out to pull him along. O'Toole kicked an Indian rug out of place in the center of the wooden floor. Underneath it was a trapdoor with a string handle. O'Toole tugged it open, knelt and felt for something. There was a click and a light went on, illuminating a ladder to the cellar below.

"It's storage," he said. "Get down there and stay there."

Shoving Maragato down in front of him, Chris squeezed through the narrow opening. O'Toole replaced the trapdoor and rug, then turned to see Lydia and five husky Visitor soldiers throw his front door open and stride in. With a swallow, he prepared to make the best of things. "Hello, can I help you?"

"Yes, you can," Lydia said evenly. "You're Mr. O'Toole, I presume?"

"Yes, ma'am, and who might you be?"

"You don't really need to know that, now do you?" she answered, holding her hand laser aimed at his chest.

"No, I suppose not."

"I'm here to arrest Michael Donovan and Ham Tyler as enemies of the occupation forces. Hand them over."

O'Toole spread his hands. "I'm sorry but I don't know what you're referring to, or whom."

Lydia turned to one of her soldiers, who was operating a hand-held scanning mechanism, sweeping the device back and forth across the room. "Two life forms unaccounted for," the officer said. He and Lydia were the only ones not wearing helmets.

"Where are they?"

"There's another level below this one, Commander."

Lydia turned back to O'Toole. "Where are they hiding?"

"They're not hiding, Lydia. And neither of them is Donovan or Tyler. I'm afraid there's been some sort of mistake."

She signaled two of the guards, who moved quickly to clamp solid grips onto O'Toole's arms. "Now then, where are they? How do we get to them?"

O'Toole slid the rug aside again, revealing the door in the floorboards. "They're just two of my workmen down there, checking my stock of supplies."

"Open it," Lydia ordered. One trooper pulled the door up while two others pointed their weapons down the ladder.

"Come up—*now*—humans," Lydia said. "You won't be harmed. We just want to question you."

After a moment, Chris emerged from the cellar, followed by Maragato. Lydia looked right at Maragato with no noticeable sign of recognition.

"Inventory's all done, boss," Chris said to O'Toole.

"Is that really what you were doing down there?" Lydia said.

"Yes, Commander," O'Toole quickly replied. "I told you neither of them was Donovan or Tyler."

"That's true, they're not," the Visitor said. She looked questioningly at her assistant, who frowned as he made three slow adjustments to his sensing device. "Anything, Lieutenant?"

He shook his head. "No, Commander. Just these two."

Without another word, Lydia spun on her heel and marched out onto the street. The shock troopers exited after her. When they'd gone, Chris closed the door.

"Son of a bitch, that was close," Faber said. "I can't believe she didn't recognize you, Maragato."

"The disguise—"

"—ain't that good. You're still Oriental and she's looking for an Oriental prisoner, but she didn't even look twice at you. I can't figure what the hell's going on around here. How did they find us?"

O'Toole nodded, wondering. "This was the first place they went, wasn't it? Why here?"

Chris stared pointedly at the Japanese. "Got any answers you'd care to contribute, Maragato?"

Lydia walked quickly to her skyfighter. James waited in the cockpit for her and she climbed in. All around the town, the shock troopers had deployed in weapons-ready guard positions. There were no townspeople to be seen, except in windows and doorways.

"Donovan's not there," Lydia said angrily.

"Who was?"

"Maragato and one of the other resistance criminals."

"Lydia, why don't we take them now? At least that way we're assured of having something for our efforts."

The security commander whirled on her aide. "Are you questioning my strategy, James? This habit you've developed is becoming increasingly tiresome."

"I'm sorry, Lydia," he said hastily. "I don't mean to question. I'm just concerned that nothing else goes wrong. If we have to face Diana empty-handed again . . ." His voice trailed off weakly.

Lydia took a deep breath to calm herself. "I appreciate your concern, even though we both know you're largely concerned with your own position should things, as you so gently put it, 'go wrong.' You chose to cast your fate with mine, James. I have no intention of watching my own career go up in a puff of smoke—so you needn't worry about yours."

He managed a wan smile as she continued.

"Do I have to remind you that it was I who proposed implanting a locator device in Maragato's body? If not for my foresight, we wouldn't even be this close to success. Put simply, we would have *no* chance for success. Now we do."

"That's true, Commander, but I still don't see why—"

"No, you really don't, do you?" Lydia shook her head sadly. "Maybe I overestimated you, James. Well, that doesn't matter right now. What does matter is that this town is under our control. This resistance fighter can't get away from us. Michael Donovan and Ham Tyler are somewhere in this area—it's only a matter of time until we get them. Tyler and Donovan don't know what *we* know, and they don't know that Maragato is actually one of my agents in human skin casing. As long as they think he's the real article—a valuable intelligence resource to be returned to the battle against the evil Visitors—they'll be back for him, and for their other friend, no matter what. These two are the bait that'll lure Donovan and Tyler to me."

As she spoke, she opened the fingers of her left hand wide. "And when they're here, we'll have what we want." She snapped her hand closed in an instant and smiled.

Donovan shook his head and got to his feet. "My God, Lydia *is* crazy if she thought of that."

Barry handed the holo-reader and cassette back to Donovan. "Keep this in case you need to refer to it again."

"Why did you do this report?" Tyler said sharply. "Why didn't you come up with something that would've told her the whole thing was impossible?"

"Because a large part of my value to you is my credibility—the fact that she believes my truthfulness. If I lose that, I lose my access to important data and planning. Just coming here may put my position in jeopardy."

"It may put your *life* in jeopardy," Donovan said. "We appreciate that, even if Tyler forgets to say it."

Barry shrugged. "We're all in danger, but the biggest danger is if my people succeed in taking over more of your planet. Our few lives don't mean much compared to the magnitude of that threat."

"Donovan," Annie called from the horses, "you about ready to go? If we want to get back before dark, we better start riding."

Donovan looked at his watch. "Where the hell is Grant? His people should've been here by now. If we don't—"

He was interrupted by a two-note chime from one of Barry's utility pockets. The Visitor took out his hand-held communicator and activated it.

"Hello, Barry—this is Teri. I know I wasn't supposed to contact you unless an emergency came up. Well, we've got one," said the female voice from the device's tiny speaker.

"What is it?" Barry asked.

"Four of Lydia's skyfighters—"

Barry's face furrowed in alarm. "Here?"

"Yes. Don't worry, they didn't spot me—I was on the ground when I saw them on my scanners. They landed in the town near here. Should I pick you up now?"

"No! Under *no* circumstances lift off. We're not in danger up here, not as long as we stay away from the town. You stay hidden. You may be our—what's that human expression?"

"Ace in the hole," Tyler said.

Barry nodded. "Ace in the hole. Keep communications to a minimum, Teri. Vital messages only. We'll have to assess the situation from up here. Barry out."

He cut the circuit and put the communicator away, then turned to his human companions.

"There's another expression," Tyler said. "Up a creek without a paddle."

Chris sat calmly near the window, feet up on the sill, gun resting in his lap, like a cowboy waiting for the bad guys to ride into town. But the bad guys were already there and the waiting was to see just what they were going to do. O'Toole paced behind him while Maragato sat in the rocking chair in the corner.

"*Attention!*" A voice from a loudspeaker shattered the quiet that lay like a glaze over the town. It was a male Visitor voice, its alien vibrato resonating clearly.

Chris cracked the curtains open. In the street, a small land rover moved slowly away from a slightly larger skyfighter, a vessel with a cargo bay in the rear, its access door still open. The rover couldn't have emerged more than a minute or two ago. The vehicle had a slit running all the way around its waistline, for viewing as well as shooting. It was about the size and height of a minivan and Chris couldn't tell if it had wheels or tracks. Whatever made it move was hidden under body armor extending to within a couple of inches of the ground.

"*Attention!*" the Visitor voice repeated. "*We have occupied this town. We know that fugitives from justice are being harbored here, and we demand that they be turned over to us. If you comply, we will leave, causing no damage to property or residents.*"

Chris rose from the chair and opened the door. Then, with O'Toole just behind him, he ventured out onto the covered porch. Other people were doing the same up and down the block. The red-uniformed shock troopers were posted in groups of twos and threes along the town's main street. They stood at attention as the rover vehicle stopped at the center of town. A different, commanding voice came from the speaker.

"*This is Lydia, security commander of the Visitor fleet. The criminals being harbored somewhere in your town are*

Michael Donovan and Ham Tyler. They have interfered with legitimate Visitor activities, with our efforts to govern fairly those areas of the planet for which we're responsible. Your own authorities have designated them as dangerous criminals to be killed on sight."

"That friggin' liar," Chris growled.

"We, on the other hand, believe all criminals can be rehabilitated to serve a valuable role in society. We only wish to help these two criminals take their places as constructive members of your society. But make no mistake— right now, they are dangerous undesirables and we will stop at nothing to hunt them down and take them into custody. We invite you to voluntarily turn them over to us. We give you thirty of your minutes to do so. At the end of that time, if Donovan and Tyler have not been given to us, we will collect twenty hostages from among your people. These hostages will be considered accomplices in the continuing criminal behavior of Donovan and Tyler, and they will be executed here in the center of your town. This will take place near dark. We will then let you think through the night about what has happened, and at dawn, we will give you one more chance to turn over the fugitives. Failure to do so will result in the apprehension and execution of twenty more accomplices every two hours until the criminals are handed to our forces—or until you have no more people left in Crow's Fork. This is by order of Diana, supreme commander, carried out by Lydia, security cadré commander." There was a pause. *"Oh, and I caution you not to attempt to escape. A substantial Visitor force surrounds your entire town. We also have electronic surveillance set up. Escape is impossible. Your only choice is to comply with justice—or else you will be inviting death."*

A bolt of fury ran through Chris as he stepped back inside O'Toole's house. He checked his watch.

"Do you think she means what she says?" O'Toole asked.

"We'll know in about twenty-nine minutes."

Chapter 11

In each residence and place of business in the little mountain town, eyes watched clocks. In the barbershop, with its three chairs, Mr. Post still held the scissors in his hands. He'd been cutting young Mark Cooke's hair when the Visitors made their announcement. The teenager was still sitting in the chair, the striped cloth still tied behind his neck, the front of it still covered by the blond hair Mr. Post had snipped.

In the general store, R. J. Penroy's cornflakes still sat on the floor where he'd been unloading the big shipping cartons and putting the new cereal boxes on the shelf. He'd only added those shop-for-yourself shelves a little over a year ago. It wasn't like a suburban supermarket with aisles and aisles of goods, and those guide signs hanging at the end of each row just so a person could tell whether he was anywhere near the products he'd come in to buy. Penroy had moved first to the front door when the aliens talked to the town, then to the counter to huddle with Mrs. Rollins, who was in her sixties and had a bad heart, and pretty young Stacy Prentiss, who was from an even smaller town than Crow's Fork and had married Bill Prentiss, the carpenter and wood worker. They dressed a little like hippies from the flower-power days, Penroy thought, but they were a nice young couple. And while Stacy waited here, she didn't know if her husband had made it home from a job in Northville, twenty miles away. She didn't know if he was safe. Penroy wished she could know.

The garage door at Stanley Polowitz's gas station was closed now, but it had been open less than a half hour ago. Stanley, a skinny, bowlegged fellow in his forties who was a fine mechanic, had been doing his usual dozen things at once, getting Edwin Lynch's sedan ready to be taken home, answering the phones, pouring waste oil into the proper barrel for disposal, sorting parts into their proper bins, tossing sawdust onto the slick underneath the pickup stuck on the lift overnight until he could get the brake parts he needed from the Chevy dealer two towns over. Stanley and Edwin had drifted to the front of the garage when the ultimatum came booming from the alien vehicle in the middle of town. They listened, watched, and closed the garage door when it was over. Edwin Lynch wanted to hurry home, but Stanley talked him out of it—it wasn't safe to go out into the street with all those Visitor soldiers. They might just grab a few home-going hostages early, if it suited them. Who was to stop them?

Families were split up in this way all over the little town. But almost no one was alone. That was the way things were in Crow's Fork. Everybody knew everybody. Not everybody *liked* everybody. But they were a tolerant group, and they pitched in when someone needed help. Now they all needed help, and neighbors huddled with neighbors. In garages and general stores and barbershops. Near doors and windows, but inside familiar places, not out on the streets suddenly made unfamiliar by the presence of these invaders from another planet.

They huddled. And they waited. And they watched clocks and looked at wristwatches. They listened to see if anyone tried to give the Visitors what they wanted, these two men who were supposed to be criminals. Two men no one even knew in Crow's Fork.

No one but Frank O'Toole, and he didn't have them.

The thirty minutes were up. Out on the street, Lydia nodded to a handful of red-uniformed shock troopers gathered around her. They fanned out to join squads of soldiers waiting nearby. In lines of five, they spread through the town like crimson tentacles reaching to grab fear-riddled victims. They advanced on houses, on shops, on the barbershop and the general store. In the lengthening shadows of late afternoon, the Visitors collected their hostages.

"Hey, where's Alex?" Annie asked. The sun would be setting soon, and she'd been seeing to the horses while Ham, Donovan, and Barry tried to figure out what to do next.

"Who cares?" Ham said.

Donovan gave him a chilling glare. "I don't know, Annie. We kind of lost track of things about ten seconds after Barry's pilot called us."

"You're not going to want to leave in the next few minutes, are you?" she asked.

"I don't think so," Donovan said. "We're probably safer up here. Plus they don't know we're here, so we've got an element of surprise that may come in handy."

Annie nodded. "Okay. Well, I'm gonna take a quick look around and see if I can find him. If we want to camp here for the night, we've got bedrolls and a little food. I packed 'em, just in case."

Donovan grinned. "You're a good guide. We'll be okay."

Annie left and Donovan turned to Tyler. "You're a real bastard, you know that?"

"Yeah, I know. So what?"

Alex had wandered off to think, and soon found himself following a shallow, meandering brook. Golden bars of light filtered through the leaves as the sun slipped closer to the horizon. He stopped to listen to the sounds of the woods—birds, squirrels, branches bending and rustling——and the whine of spinning tires. He ducked low to peer under tree limbs and tried to peg the direction of the sound. He moved stealthily toward it, still following the stream. After a hundred yards or so, he saw a washed-out plank bridge and a dirty jeep stuck on one bank of the stream. It was wider and deeper here, which was why the bridge had been built in the first place. Two men were standing thigh deep in water, trying to push the vehicle, and a woman sat in the driver's seat.

"Hey, need a hand?" Alex called.

The driver let up on the accelerator and her companions stopped pushing. "Yeah," said one of the men, a balding blond with an unkempt beard. The other man was younger and much taller. The woman's face was dirt streaked, and all of them seemed edgy.

"Yeah," the blond man repeated. "What are you doing out here?"

Alex carefully stepped down to the water's edge. "I was about to ask you the same question. This bridge's been out for months—nobody goes this way."

"That's why we're going this way. Don't you know what's going on in town?" the woman said, a tremor in her voice.

"You mean Crow's Fork? No, we've been out here all day."

"Who's we?" the tall man asked.

"Oh, three others, up at the mine. What's going on in town?"

The three travelers exchanged nervous looks. "Visitors," the blond man finally said. "They landed, looking for two guys—Donovan and Tyler, I think their names were."

Alex started at the mention of the names, then tried to cover his interest. "Yeah? What do they want 'em for?"

The blond man shrugged. "Not sure—we don't live in town, we're from outside, but a friend of ours called us and warned us to get as far away as we can. Said people in town are stuck, prisoners. That's why we're taking the back roads—don't want any lizard patrols to spot us. You and your friends better forget about going back into town if that's where you're headed."

"They didn't get these two guys?" Alex asked cautiously.

"Nope," said the woman at the wheel. "They're going to take hostages and kill them if the town doesn't hand them over."

"Really?" Alex started backing up the grassy bank.

"Hey! I thought you were going to help us!" the blond man shouted angrily.

"I—I can't. Gotta tell my friends about this. Sorry," he called back as he scrambled up to the trail and broke into a trot.

But he didn't return to the mine. He kept running until he got to the gravel two-lane, saw a sign that said, "Crow's Fork—2 Miles," and jogged in that direction.

Annie sat on a tree stump by the side of the trail, her knees hugged to her chest.

"Hey." It was Ham's voice, and she looked up briefly, then hunched back into a ball.

He came over and knelt in front of her. "You okay?"

She shrugged.

"Talkative mood, eh, Halsey?"

She shrugged again.

"Donovan told me I was a bastard. I agreed with him. But you always knew that, right?" He paused, but there was still no response. "Look, Alex knows these woods as well as you do, so he's probably fine. Hey, if you want to be alone, I'll go." He started to move away slowly. "If you want the company, just say so." He took another step back.

Annie spoke without looking up. "Why did you come after me?"

"To apologize."

"You haven't done it yet."

"Huh? Oh, yeah, I guess I forgot. Hey, I'm sorry for what I said, for picking on your boyfriend."

Now she looked at him. "Thanks," she said without expression.

"Don't mention it."

They were quiet for a long moment, eyes still on each other. "Hey, Tyler," she said, crooking a finger at him, beckoning. He came closer, bent over, and she reached up, grabbed his collar, pulled him down, and kissed him softly. He straightened, his brow furrowed.

"Halsey, what was that for?"

She tilted her head quizzically. "Damned if I know." She unfolded her legs and linked her arm in his. They started back for the camp.

The four Visitor skyfighters were gathered in a circle, like some futuristic wagon train. Each was ringed by helmeted guards, and cabin lights were visible through the windows of one—the command ship, where Lydia sat in the rear compartment, a makeshift field office set up in the cramped space between the cockpit in front and the gunner's nest aft. James approached Lydia's craft and ducked low to enter the open hatch.

"Commander," he said, "those hostages have been gathered."

"Good. I want to get rid of them while we still have enough daylight for people to see what will hapeen to *them* if they don't cooperate." Her boots had been removed and they stood next to her seat. She reached down and pulled them on. James stepped aside and they both went out in the cooling early evening air.

Twenty frightened people stood in a haphazard group some distance away, and Lydia gave herself a moment to scan these humans. There was an even mixture of male and female, young and adult. She took her communicator in hand, touched a button, and spoke; her voice reverberated from a speaker in her skyfighter, and the entire town could hear.

"This is Lydia, security cadré commander. Your time is up, and you have forced us to take an action we would prefer not to take. Because the two criminal fugitives have not been given to us, we must kill twenty of your people—twenty accomplices to the crimes of Donovan and Tyler. They are enemies of the state. We—"

Lydia's speech was interrupted by a shout from a guard behind her. She spun in place and headlights flashed in her eyes. She was momentarily blinded, and when she turned again, eyes shaded, vision cleared, she saw several of her troopers running toward a car that was careening erratically toward the Visitor rover vehicle. The guards had their rifles aimed and shouted for the car to stop.

Lydia advanced a few steps, but James held her back. She shook loose, but it was too late for her to do anything other than bellow at her officers, *"Shoot now!"*

The troopers complied, four laser bolts surging at the runaway car split seconds apart. The windshield shattered and the metal tore and the car swerved suddenly and rammed a tree. Then it exploded. By the light of the licking flames, Lydia peered into the passenger compartment. James stood beside her.

"There's no driver in there," Lydia said.

"Are you sure?"

They took a couple of steps closer, their artificial skins serving as protection against the heat. James peered in for himself. "You're right. Just what do these humans think they're doing?"

"Oh, they know what they're doing—sabotage." She marched back to where the prisoners were being held. "Arrange them in a line," she barked. The shock troopers followed the order, then backed up into a line of their own. Lydia spoke into her communicator again, continuing her broadcast.

"People of Crow's Fork, I want you to see the rewards for criminal behavior." She turned to the makeshift firing squad. *"Fire."*

The troops pulled the triggers, and their rifles shot continuous beams instead of bolts. At the instant the beams hit their targets, an unearthly wail went up, like a ghostly, screaming wind.

The sound made Chris shudder. He knew that the victims only had a second to cry out before the energy of the lasers killed them. Now only a muddy red fireball existed where human bodies had been moments before as the people were vaporized before the eyes of the rest of the town. One of the Visitors called out a cease-fire order and the weapons stopped. The echoing sound lingered, then faded. And then there was nothing where twenty innocent people had stood.

In the face of that horror, Chris's mind wandered to the

act of defiance that had preceded it. Who'd been responsible for that out-of-control car? Someone in town was determined not to take Visitor atrocities without fighting back.

Alex covered his face, cold tears on his cheeks. Hidden by bushes and trees, he lay on his belly on a hillock overlooking Crow's Fork. His mind reeled—those creatures had just killed a score of innocent people in cold blood—and he was actually going to brazenly march into town and demand to see their commander?

Are you nuts, Alex? He answered his own silent question, out loud: "Must be."

He tried to shake the numbness out of his limbs. He got to his knees, leaning his hands on the grass. He felt nothing. He willed his feet to move ahead, down the hillside.

Down to a place that had turned, in less than a day, into a close approximation of hell.

O'Toole sat limply on his desk, shoulders hunched forward, jaw slack. "She just burned them down, twenty lives gone—like matches tossed into a campfire." His voice was hushed, empty.

Chris stood just inside the open door, the fading light from outside framing his hair. "Look, O'Toole, I know you knew those people. Hell, we've all lost friends to the Visitors—if not this time, the first time they invaded."

Eyes hollow, O'Toole lifted his head to focus on Chris. "No, no, I never lost anybody I cared about. Not in the first war, not in this one—not until you people brought your goddamned war up here with you. Nobody cared about this place, nobody bothered us. Your war was your war, not mine. Those twenty innocent people died because of you and Maragato and Tyler and Donovan. God knows where they are—maybe Alex and Annie are dead too."

"O'Toole, listen to me—"

"No, you listen to me. You get out of here and you take him with you."

"We can't. We gotta wait. We gotta see what's going down next and we gotta get Lydia and the Visitors back for what they did." Chris came closer to O'Toole, hoping he could persuade him if he could look the man in the eye.

When Chris was seven feet from the door, Maragato broke for the opening. Chris abruptly changed direction, and his feet skidded on the wooden floor. He dove and grabbed Maragato's leg, and they both tumbled into the wall. The little Japanese spy had inhuman strength, and it suddenly dawned on Chris that he *wasn't* human at all. He decided to change wrestling tactics. Instead of grappling for a superior position, Chris drove his fingers into Maragato's face, tearing at the flesh.

"O'Toole, help me!" Chris yelled. "This guy ain't human."

Chris clawed with all the strength in his left hand while he tried to maintain some control over his writhing adversary with his right.

O'Toole watched, still not moving, until he heard a guttural snarl rise out of the struggle. Down to his bones, he knew that sound didn't come from a human throat. For a fleeting instant, he saw something long and greenish-black snake out of Maragato's mouth. A stream of sparkling spittle issued from that nightmarish tongue and Chris yelped in pain, throwing up a hand to protect his eyes. He let go of Maragato, who rose up ready to finish Chris off. It was the instant of advantage he needed to—

The chair crashed across Maragato's head.

O'Toole had swung from his heels and followed through with stunning force. Maragato flipped backward and crumpled to the floor, still conscious but dazed. Chris leaped to his feet and kicked Maragato's face, the impact making a squishing thud. The alien slumped down in a heap. Chris staggered and O'Toole caught him, holding him under the arms until he was steady.

Breathing heavily, Chris drew his gun from its holster, released the safety, and approached Maragato. The skin on his face was gouged, but there was no blood.

O'Toole's eyes bulged in shock as he watched Chris dig his nails into the torn flesh, then peel it back, revealing the dark, scale-covered face of a Visitor!

O'Toole watched the lipless gash for a mouth, the slitted nostrils, the reptilian tongue lolling as the *thing* that had been Kyoshi Maragato struggled back to consciousness. O'Toole couldn't pull his staring eyes away from the Visitor.

With his gun trained on Maragato, Chris backed up and came to O'Toole. "We never had the real Maragato. When Lydia kidnapped the guy from Japan, she had him replaced with a fake."

"But why? You were never supposed to get your hands on those agents again. They were going to be sent to Diana and probably killed. So why go to the trouble of creating an impostor?"

Chris shrugged. "Only Lydia knows, but I have a good guess. While the three agents were in custody, they were together. This fake could get buddy-buddy with the other two and find out quite a bit. Or maybe she was covering her ass in case we really did manage to break 'em loose before Diana got 'em. Who the hell knows? But something else is bothering me."

"What?"

"The timing of this so-called top-secret plan Barry was supposed to pass to Donovan and Tyler. It just happens to pop up right after we embarrass the pants off Lydia by stealing VIP prisoners out from under her nose."

"What do you think—that maybe the whole thing was some kind of setup?"

Chris shook his head. "I don't know—too many blank spaces at this point. But I'm damn well gonna fill some of 'em in before this is all over. You still don't want to get involved, O'Toole?"

"I guess I am involved, whether I like it or not."

"Yeah, you are. Jesus, I sure could use a beer. Oh, I forgot. How about a glass of orange juice?"

Lydia looked up from her small desk in the skyfighter. James was just entering with a human—Alex.

"Sorry to disturb you, Lydia, but we have a prisoner."

Alex tried to shake loose from the grip James held on

him, to no avail. "Hey, I'm not a prisoner. I came here voluntarily."

Lydia's face formed a dubious frown. "Oh, and why is that, human?"

"Because I have some information I think you might want to hear."

"What information could you possibly have for me?"

Alex straightened to his full height, trying to exude confidence. "I know where Mike Donovan and Ham Tyler are."

The words took a second to register, then Lydia stiffened. She stood and came up to Alex face to face. "You do? All right, I'm listening."

Alex glanced pointedly at James's hands on his arms, pinning them to his sides. "Uh—"

"Release him," Lydia snapped.

Once free, Alex shook himself to restore the circulation, rubbing his biceps muscles and wincing.

"Well?" Lydia prodded impatiently.

"Not so fast, Lydia. We have to discuss—"

There was a fireball of brightness from outside as a blast of shimmering heat rushed in the hatchway and a bursting explosion shook Lydia's skyfighter to its frame. James, Lydia, and Alex all had to reach for a bulkhead to keep from being knocked over. The commander pushed past her prisoner and her junior officer and took one step out of the ship. Wordlessly, she watched as one of the other skyfighters was engulfed in a roiling fist of flame.

A grimy shock trooper rushed up to her, his helmet askew and his uniform streaked with dirt. "Commander! Someone blew up the—"

She silenced him with a withering stare. "I know what's been blown up. If you and your men don't find the culprits and prevent any other acts of sabotage, I may have you all executed in place of the hostages in the morning. Do I make myself clear?"

"Yes, Commander, yes!"

The shaken trooper backed off, bowing his head obsequiously. Lydia stepped back into her ship. James and Alex got out of her way. "I thought these were crack forces you brought down here, Lieutenant," she said harshly.

"They were—I mean, they *are*, Lydia," James said.

Alex smiled condescendingly. "What's the matter—are humans tougher than you expected them to be?"

Lydia whirled on him. "Don't get chatty with me, human. Or information or no, I'll kill you myself, right here and now. With my bare hands."

Alex shrank back into a corner. Lydia seemed pleased to have reestablished superiority over this sniveling human at least. "Now, then, tell me the information about Donovan and Tyler. *Now*."

"Like I said, not so fast," Alex said, thrusting his shoulders back with an air of authority. *Two can play that game*, he thought. "What's in it for me? You obviously want these two real bad, if you were willing to put yourself and your troops out in the open like this, killing innocent civilians to boot. You're taking a lot of risks, lady."

"So are you, human, so are you."

"Maybe—but I think you'll bargain for this sort of info. Am I right?"

Lydia sat back in her seat, drumming her fingers on the computer console. "Yes, I suppose you are. What's your name?"

"Alex. Alex Kramer. First, I want you to leave the people of Crow's Fork alone."

"How noble of you, Alex."

He flared. "I'm not kidding. They don't know anything about Donovan and Tyler. You could kill them all and you'd never find out what you want to know. I'm the only one who can tell you."

"Then tell me."

"Oh, no. I need to know more about what I get for turning these jokers in. I want money, and I want a place to live, a safe place where you people won't do anything to me. That means up north, in *human*-occupied territory."

Lydia laughed derisively. "What do I look like, a banker and real-estate agent?"

"Oh, you can get that stuff for me if you really want to. Just go through Nathan Bates. He's got money and land."

"I see you have this well thought out."

"Yeah, I sure do, Lydia. I'll give you until dawn tomorrow to at least get me the money."

"How much?"

"Five hundred thousand dollars." He thought the request would provoke a reaction, but all she did was smile.

"I'd really like you to tell me where they are now."

"No. My way or no way."

"Fine. And as a gesture of good faith, I won't take any more hostages overnight." Her voice sharpened to a stiletto sharpness. "But make no mistake—if you're not forthcoming with the information by first light tomorrow, I'll not only kill more of your friends, you'll be first in line."

"Good night, Lydia."

"Good night."

He left the skyfighter. "Take two men with you and follow him," Lydia ordered. "Don't let our friend Alex out of your sight."

James nodded and went outside. Lydia was left alone, gritting her teeth in anger and frustration.

Chapter 12

Julie rested here chin on her folded arms and stretched forward across the table. She watched the Art Deco clock on the wall; the chandelier light glinted off the golden rays that spread out from its face like sunbeams. Alone in the basement at Club Creole, she listened as footsteps echoed softly in the outside passageway. She looked up as the door opened. It was Elias, now back in white pants and a white shirt open at the neck.

"Clock watching?"

She smiled weakly. "I guess."

"Mind if I join you?"

"If you want."

He sat down at her table. "Actually, no, I don't want to, but nobody's been able to talk you *out* of it. Look, Julie, I'm sure they're okay."

She sat up. Her eyes were red and he could guess that she'd been crying.

"Why does everyone always say that?" she wanted to know. "I mean we're all adults, and we all know they should've been back hours ago. So why does everyone keep telling me they're okay?" Her voice caught, and she quickly covered her eyes, hoping to head off the tears she knew were waiting to fall.

Elias gently touched her shoulder and she leaned against him, too weary even to embrace. He stroked her hair. "We're all worried, babe. But you know we can't do anything until morning. They'll be back by then, or we'll get some word from 'em.''

Julie looked up. "And if they're not, or we haven't heard a thing?"

"Then we'll go take a look."

With a deep sigh, Julie slumped forward again, burying her face, her fingers kneading the base of her neck. Elias stood over her and took over the massage. Julie turned her head slightly.

"Are we racists, Elias?"

"Huh? You mean you white folks?"

"No," she said. "I'm serious. I mean all of us."

He stopped the massage, his face perplexed. "You lost me, babe."

She rested her head on one elbow, trying to make some sense of her private thoughts. "We hate the Visitors because of what they are. We meet a lizard, we automatically distrust him." She caught herself, annoyance evident in her expression. "Damn! Listen to me—I just called them lizards."

"Well, that's what they *are*."

Julie shook her head vigorously. "No! They're reptilian."

"What's the diff?"

"The difference between calling me 'white' and calling me 'Whitey.' Or the difference between 'Negro' and 'nigger.' I can call you a bastard, and that's okay. But if I call you a 'black bastard,' *that's* racist! Now do you see what I mean?"

"Not really—"

Julie balled her fists up in frustration. "Damn. Why can't I think of the right way to say this?"

He began massaging her neck and shoulders again. "Hey, relax, Jule. Maybe I'm just a little slow. What about Willie?"

"What do you mean?"

"Well, we don't hate him, and he's a Visitor."

"We don't hate him *now*, but do you remember when we first met him? Remember when he saved your dad in that factory accident? Well, the next time you saw him was at your brother's funeral—and you and your father wanted to kill him, right there on the street, just because he was a Visitor."

Elias stopped rubbing her shoulders as the memory came back to him. "Ben," he said, softly mouthing his dead brother's name. "It wasn't 'cause it was Willie—I didn't even know who he was then. It was 'cause the lizards killed Ben."

"But Willie didn't," Julie said gently. "But you still hated him because he was *one of them*."

"How can you blame us for feelin' this way? It's like Jews being afraid of Germans during the war, all Germans, not just Hitler and the dudes in the S.S. How were they supposed to know which were the good Germans, or even if there *were* any good Germans?"

"But aren't we better than that?" Julie asked, her voice rising in intensity. "Aren't we better than the German who hated *all* Jews because he was told to? Aren't we less frightened than the Jews who were afraid to fight back?"

"No! Why should we be? People are people, Julie, ain't they? Besides, there *is* a difference. We try real hard to ask questions first and shoot later, even if it means risking our butts. Hell, considering we didn't start this war, I think that's pretty damn reasonable of us."

"I guess. . . ." she ended, but doubt hung in her voice.

"And some of my best friends are Visitors!" he said half jokingly. He saw the beginning of a smile on Julie's tired face. "That's better! Now come on upstairs. While we were gone all day, my chefs cooked up some real special stuff. Real *expensive* special stuff. They always do it when I'm not around. I'd fire 'em for insubordination, but they cook too damn good."

Julie's smile broadened, and Elias pulled her to her feet.

"We just closed," he continued. "I chased the slow-eating dudes out the front door, and I got leftovers! Some of the others are hanging out and they're waiting for us. So let's get up there before they give up and don't leave nothin' for us. Much as it pains me to say this, it's on the house."

"Booze too?"

Elias backed away, feigning horror. "What do I look like, an idiot?"

"How did they cover up your real voice?" Chris asked, standing over a very securely tied "Maragato." It was hard to think of him by that name as he sat on a cot, the lower half of his human face now removed.

"Surgical alterations," he said, still sounding fully human. "An electronic implant filters out the extra sounds produced by our multiple vocal apparatus."

As he spoke, his fingers—hidden down behind his back—were working carefully on the rope knots that bound him.

"I want to know what Lydia was gonna do with you," Chris said.

"Oh, really now, you don't expect me to tell you that, do you?"

Chris leveled the barrel of his gun at Maragato's eyes. "Yeah, as a matter of fact I do."

The interrogation was cut off by sounds from the main room out front.

"What the hell are you doing here?" O'Toole's voice said, surprised by someone's arrival.

Chris went to the doorway between the two rooms and saw Alex, by himself. "Where the hell have you been and where are Mike and Ham?"

"Geez, don't I even get a 'glad to see you'?" Alex pouted.

"Do you mind if I beat his face in, O'Toole?" Chris said mildly.

"Whoa, hey, nice greeting," Alex said. "Relax. The others are safe and they're still up at the mine. Grant and his people never met us up there. Barry, the Visitor guy, did."

"Grant was probably scared off by the Visitors landing here in town," Chris said. "He hadda come by here on his way up to the mountain. Why didn't the others come down with you?"

"Well, they don't know I'm here. See, I went for a walk,

and I ran into some people who told me what was going on here."

"Did you tell Mike and Ham?" Chris asked.

"No. They already knew the Visitors'd landed here, because Barry's pilot called us. But we didn't know anything about the hostages or that stuff. Didn't seem any purpose in my going back up and telling 'em that—they were planning to stay put for a while. But I thought I should come back here and see if you all needed any help. Hey, where's Maragato?"

Chris gestured toward the back room. Alex went to the blanket divider hanging in the doorway and moved it aside. He saw the Visitor who used to be Maragato. "My God!"

"Precisely," O'Toole said.

"I better get back there and keep an eye on him," Chris said. He brushed past Alex, who waited until the resistance fighter was in the other room, then took his boss aside.

"O'Toole, we've gotta talk—privately, without him," Alex whispered. "You and me are the only ones down here who know where Donovan and Tyler are."

"I'd like to keep it that way."

"We do that, we could wind up very dead. Lydia means business."

O'Toole closed his eyes. "I know, I saw what she did."

"So did I. We can save more people from being slaughtered."

The big Irishman narrowed his eyes. "What the hell are you saying, Alex?"

"We can tell Lydia. We can lead her right to 'em. I came into town to talk to her, and I—"

O'Toole whirled and clamped a meaty hand around the younger man's throat. "You stupid son of a bitch!"

"Hey, I didn't tell her anything! Let go!" Alex croaked. The grip loosened, but the hand stayed in place, as if inviting Alex to continue, but at his own peril. He swallowed hard. "She's willing to bargain—we can get money, land, go where it's safe, where we don't have to risk getting murdered by Visitors or caught in the crossfire by rebels. Interested?"

O'Toole leaned in until there was less than an inch between his nose and Alex's. "Go on."

"I think I know how you feel. I think we both want to avoid getting tangled up in this. Let Annie do it if she wants to, she's been doing this kind of stuff for years. If she wants to recapture past glory with Ham Tyler and make believe she's back in Central America, let her do it without us! They're crazy, these people in the resistance. They don't care who gets killed, who gets in the way. We know they're never going to defeat the Visitors, so why shouldn't we get a little something and get away from the fighting?"

"Are you quite finished?" O'Toole said through clenched jaws.

"Yeah."

"You stupid little bastard," the Irishman hissed. "That's a Visitor in there, and he's the reason all this happened. He and those aliens outside. I should tell Chris Faber what you've just told me and let him tear you apart."

Alex hung limply in O'Toole's grip. "I—I didn't tell her anything. I was going to decide and tell her in the morning."

"The only reason I believe you is because you're so damned scared right now I don't think it would occur to you to lie. If you decide you want to be a traitor come sunrise, that's your choice. But I should tell you, it'll leave *me* no choice but to kill you before you can tell Lydia anything. You're going to stay here tonight. My guess is, Lydia's got people watching you anyway, so there's no place you could run to. You think it over, and you tell me in the morning. Meanwhile"—he smiled threateningly—"this chat will be our little secret." He reluctantly removed his fingers from Alex's neck.

After a sleepless night waiting for Barry to return to the Mother Ship, Zachary visited the giant vessel's upper observation deck. It was nearly dawn down in California, the disk of the sun visible in the east, rising over the ridge of mountains running from north to south on this part of the continent. Zachary could see the sun from the Mother Ship's mile-high altitude, but it would be awhile before the light reached those on the ground.

Use your judgment, Barry had told him. Well, in his judgment, Barry should have been back long ago. Something must have gone terribly wrong, and it would be up to him to make certain the Los Angeles resistance group had the information they'd need about Lydia's plans. As he watched the brightness spread over the land below, his mind was already forming the precise checklist of tasks he'd have to do in order to deliver Barry's report to the humans. He'd need to secure a skyfighter—falsifying the proper permit shouldn't be much of a problem. To keep things as simple as possible this time, he wouldn't take a pilot but would fly out by himself, ostensibly to test a malfunctioning engine on a craft he'd logged in yesterday as being troublesome on its last mission.

Chapter 13

The first rays of early morning shone through the panes of Frank O'Toole's windows. O'Toole and Alex sipped cups of coffee out front, and Chris emerged from the back room to join them. O'Toole poured another steaming mug, and Chris took it, then looked straight into the younger guide's eyes. Alex immediately averted his gaze.

"Don't worry," Chris said amiably. "If I didn't kill you last night, you've got a fighting chance to get through today—*if* you've come to the right decision. If you haven't, I wouldn't sell you life insurance in the next ten minutes or so. Bad risk."

Alex turned pale.

"I told him your tale of entrepreneurship," O'Toole said.

"But you said—" Alex began to protest feebly.

O'Toole cut him off. "He had a right to know." He paused for another mouthful of coffee. "So what *have* you decided, Alex?"

The young man swallowed. "Uh, I've changed my mind. I doubt Lydia's word is much good."

"He's seen the light," Chris said sardonically.

Alex tried an intimidating glare, but it didn't work. "All I want to do now is get the hell away from here."

Chris chuckled. "Get outa here? After what you offered Lydia?"

"Sure, why not?" Alex's back was to the windows, and he noticed Chris looking outside, over Alex's shoulder.

"Did you really think they'd actually let you waltz right through their little lizard fingers?" Chris asked.

Alex's face reflected sudden dread at Chris's tone. Slowly, he turned to view what Chris was watching, and saw a squad of Visitor shock troopers forming up in the center of town. Lydia came out of her skyfighter to take command from James. The aliens' helmet visors were down to protect their light-sensitive eyes against the morning brightness, and they all carried lethal-looking laser rifles in a ready-to-fire position. They arranged themselves in a flying wedge, with Lydia safe behind the leading center of the V, and turned and marched directly toward O'Toole's place.

"Oh, hell," Alex croaked in a parched voice.

Maragato had worked religiously through the night to loosen the ropes binding his wrists and restraining them tightly behind his back. Inwardly, he'd found himself laughing at the humans' assumptions that a being with superior strength could be bound by simple ties. They'd forgotten that his human-appearing skin wasn't prone to injury when placed under stress as their biological epidermal layer was. His was a form of high-strength plastic. It took quite a lot to rip it—direct pressure with sharp points. So he'd twisted against the ropes for hours while the humans slept, and the ropes had worn thin, finally breaking silently. Then he'd reached down and undone the bindings on his legs, using one of his false fingernails like a knife. He had to admit the knots were well tied. But, after replacing the ropes in a loose facsimile of the original knots, he knew he was free to move when the moment was right.

"Got your speech all rehearsed, Alex?" Chris said mockingly.

Sweat began beading up on Alex's face. He peeked past the curtains again, hoping the Visitor group had changed direction. It hadn't.

I should run, Alex thought, plans racing crazily through

his brain. *Which way to go? Gotta get away from them—goddamn lizards!*

O'Toole and Chris kept watching out the window, and they didn't notice Alex creeping backward away from them, away from what had become a death watch.

And none of them saw "Maragato," his half-human half-alien face alight with determination, move slowly, silently through the doorway between the back room and front. He took two steps toward them, but Alex spun to flee and ran right into the Visitor. Maragato reacted first, grabbing Alex and hurling him into O'Toole, who'd turned to intercept the unexpectedly free prisoner. The big man fell flat on his back, sliding on the small rug in the center of the room. Alex skidded across the floor, nearly to the front door, then lay there, momentarily stunned. Maragato braced himself for a lunge at Chris.

The alien crouched, his leg muscles uncoiled—Chris reached under his jacket, his hand a lightning blur—Maragato in mid-air, hands shaped into killing claws—a lancing beam of sunlight glinting off the pistol as it flashed forward—finger squeezing the trigger, calm and steady—the gun firing, the puff of smoke, the dull thunder following a split later—

The hollow-tipped bullet tore into Maragato's chest and the impact slowed his dive and changed his trajectory. He fell to the floor at Chris's feet, clutching his chest, dark blood pulsing out of the wound. His breath came in shallow rasps.

Eyes darting, Chris measured the scene, but before he could move an explosion from the side of the house threw him forward. He landed on his back, wind knocked out of him, then he rolled painfully onto one elbow.

At the blast, each of Lydia's phalanx of soldiers dropped to one knee, weapon up and aimed. The explosion came from a garbage can next to O'Toole's establishment, ripping the metal can into shrapnel and sending up a tongue of flame. The fire caught the edge of the porch and crackled hungrily along the painted wood.

Lydia crouched behind her troopers, sizing up the
situation. She guessed this to be another act of sabotage,
and there was no way she was going to let it stop her from
getting to Alex Kramer, that foolish human who had dared
taunt her the night before—

—Alex Kramer, who scrambled to his feet the second
after the explosion, thanked God for this providential diver-
sion, and scuttled through the front door of the burning
house on hands and knees, driving for daylight like a foot-
ball running back.

Chris saw him go, but it was too late to do anything
except call after him: *"No, Alex, you jackass!"*

"Get him—alive!" Lydia snarled.

The shock troopers broke formation and charged after
their quarry. Panic gave Alex the head start he'd prayed for,
but it also made his coordination disappear. He slipped,
tumbled, and when he turned to face upward, the shadows
of six bulky Visitors covered him. They hauled him to his
feet as Lydia came over to him.

Chris saw the Visitors catch Alex. Staying low, he
hopped over the very dead Maragato. Smoke blew in
through the windows and door, and Chris could hear the
staccato crackle of flames as they devoured the side of the
house. His eyes teared and he wiped them with the back of
one hand, the other hand gripping his gun. He thought he
saw O'Toole coming up behind him.

"C'mon," Chris called back, "we got one chance!"

Ducking his head for one last breath of clear air, Chris
rose up and barreled shoulder first through the large window
on the side of the house away from the approaching fire. He
somersaulted out, head over heels, and landed with a
clumsy roll on the grass outside. It took a moment to still
the dizziness in his head and figure out which direction he
wanted to go—

A moment later, out of his sight, the churning flames
licked a propane gas tank on the front porch and the house

exploded into a fireball that flared high above the town like a miniature atomic burst. Heat blasted out at Chris, sucking the cool air into itself like a living thing pulling in breath.

He scrabbled to his feet and crashed headlong into the woods, putting as much distance between himself and the inferno as he could. He fell against a sturdy tree trunk, then looked back at the crumbling frame skeleton that had been a house only a minute ago. "O'Toole," he whispered. He shook his head sadly. *I liked him, even if he didn't have anything you could drink.*

Then the sounds of footsteps breaking twigs snared his attention and yanked him back to the problem at hand—survival. The sounds meant someone else was in the woods with him.

His feet barely touching the ground, Alex was dragged away from the house by the shock troopers. He turned to look over his shoulder once. The flames were already curling up to the roof and the walls were caving in. Anyone left inside was dead by now.

When he turned again, he found himself face to face with Lydia, her mouth set in an ominous expression.

"Now," she said, "you *will* tell me what you know of the whereabouts of Michael Donovan and Ham Tyler." Her reptilian tongue flicked out in anger and a threatening hiss came from her throat.

Soundlessly, Chris hunkered down amid a cluster of bushes. The branches scratched his skin, but he settled in and listened. The footsteps came closer. Whoever was producing them seemed unconcerned about being secretive. Then he heard voices—two teenagers by the sound of them.

"Jesus, Bradley, I told you it was too close to the house. It's gonna burn down the whole town."

"Better than letting the Visitors have it," Bradley said, belligerence in his voice.

Chris poised on his feet and waited. Then he peered through the leaves surrounding him until he saw blue jeans and sneakers approaching. When they'd taken three steps past him, he shook loose from the foliage and stood astride the overgrown path. "You fellas do good work, but you need a little polish."

They froze in place. The stockier one shoved a hand deep into his pants pocket, then turned with studied arrogance. Chris suppressed a grin and took this one to be Bradley.

"You ready to get blown away, sucker?" the kid said sternly.

His taller, towheaded friend rolled his eyes.

"No, are you?" Chris responded, drawing his gun.

"Bradley, cut the crap," the other boy whispered out the side of his mouth. "The gun's real."

Acceding to the request, Bradley withdrew hand from pocket and shrugged. "You're obviously not a Visitor. Since you got a gun and you're sneaking around in the woods right after O'Toole's house blew up, my guess is you got something to do with the resistance, and with this Donovan and Tyler the lizards want so bad."

Chris smile admiringly. "Good analysis, kid."

The blond boy pointed at Chris's neck. "You're also bleeding."

Chris glanced down. He hadn't thought to check for damage after departing through the window. "Dammit." It wasn't a serious cut, but the oozing blood had soaked his shirt collar, though his jacket had protected him otherwise. "That's what I get for climbing out a window without opening it first."

"I'm a med tech," the blond kid said. "I can patch you up."

Chris nodded. "Okay, thanks. And I'd like to get in on your operation, if you don't mind."

"Who said we need a partner?" Bradley said.

"Nobody. In fact, I probably couldn't have escaped if you guys hadn't come along with that bomb when you did. I owe you one. But I think we might be able to help each other. Besides, you remind me of myself when I was about your age, the way you're blowing things up."

"Oh? And what did you grow up to be?" the blond boy asked.

"CIA agent," Chris said modestly.

The boys' eyes glowed. "Okay," said the stockier boy, "let's quit standing around waiting for the Visitors to find us. We got a lot of work to do. I'm Bradley, and this is Hank."

Chris extended his hand—without the gun. "Chris Faber. Glad to meet you. Lead the way. . . ."

Bradley stepped forward and they headed deeper into the woods.

Chapter 14

Annie carefully held the branch away from herself as she stepped along the trail, then just as carefully let it snap back in Ham Tyler's face.

"You sure have a funny way of showing your gratitude," he said peevishly.

"Gratitude? For what?"

"For my coming out with you again this morning to look for your runaway boyfriend."

She stopped, turned, and kissed him quickly on the cheek. "Is that a better way?"

"Getting there. Hey, let's take a rest stop." He found a grassy spot in the shade of a stand of tall trees and plunked himself down.

Annie stood over him, shaking her head. "You're gettin' old, Tyler. You don't have the same stamina."

"Yeah, well, it's this cushy life fighting the lizards. Just doesn't keep me in shape the way covert activities for the Company used to."

She sat cross-legged next to him, her fingers playing on his knee.

"You don't seem as anxious to find your boyfriend as you were yesterday," he noted.

"Oh, you know me. I get excited and then I get rational again. I'm sure he's okay. Maybe he just got pissed off at you and decided to head back to town."

"What do we do, look for him all day?"

Annie shook her head. "Nope. We'll look a little while

132

longer, then head back to camp. If Donovan and Barry and you can figure out where we go next, then we'll go." She was quiet for a moment. "Hair's gotten a little thinner since last time, Tyler."

"You said it yourself—I'm getting old, sweetheart. I'm not the only one, though. You've got a few more wrinkles around those baby blues."

She smiled sardonically. "You're such a charmer."

He shrugged modestly. "Hey, some things never change. So, tell me, what do you see in this boyfriend of yours?"

She mulled over the question, then raised an eyebrow. "Less and less, now that I see you again." She gently grabbed his collar, pulled him close, and kissed him.

He hesitated returning it, and she backed off.

"Something wrong?" she asked.

"I'm not sure, Halsey. What if the boyfriend stumbles outa the woods and finds us?"

"He ran off without me; I don't owe him anything. Y'know, I've wanted to seduce you again for five years. Two years ago, we didn't have the time. But I swore if we ever got together again, nothing was gonna stop me."

He frowned. "Hey, I thought I seduced *you* the first time."

"You also thought it was you who saved my life. For a CIA man, you've got a lousy memory."

"Ex-CIA," he corrected.

"Oh, yeah. You know, I really thought you'd gone commercial after you beat the Visitors and opened that big-time security company."

"It was just a phase. I outgrew it."

"You and your friends were in all the papers. I almost looked you up. I was gonna make fun of you for selling out and going establishment."

"Well, if that was the only reason you were going to look me up, I'm glad you didn't."

"I've got another reason now." She closed her arms around his neck. This time there was no hesitation about joining the kiss—or continuing it. After a long time, they broke for a breath. Ham played with her hair, and Annie just smiled. Then she leaned back on the grass and pulled him over on top of her.

He resisted, going down only halfway, then stopping. "Hey, come on. There're bugs all over the place," he complained.

"You didn't mind making love outdoors in Salvador. And the bugs were a hell of a lot bigger down there."

"I was younger then—stupider too. Besides, those bugs were *so* big they could've passed for family."

"Your family, maybe," she said lightly.

"You're a real charmer too, Halsey."

"What can I say? I went to the Ham Tyler School of Etiquette." Propping herself on one elbow, she began unbuttoning Ham's shirt.

"You're not going to take no for an answer, are you?" he asked, an amused glint in his eye. He ran one hand along her firm body, from her thigh to the bare skin of her neck.

"Nope." She reached down to unbuckle his pants. "C'mon, Tyler, be young again."

"I'm being overwhelmed by superior forces."

She grinned slyly. "I may be superior, but you're not bad, if I recall correctly." She pushed him onto his back and rolled on top of him, finishing off his shirt buttons and scraping her fingernails through the hair on his chest.

They made love softly, quietly, revisiting old feelings under tentative new circumstances. Annie quickened the pace.

"Hey, slow down, Halsey," Ham whispered as she straddled him.

She bit his earlobe. "Uh-uhh. I've been patient for five years, Tyler. No time for patience now. Besides, we don't have all day."

"You're a real romantic, kid."

Her breathing quickened. "If I wasn't, I wouldn't be sittin' up here after all this time, now would I?"

He gave in to her urgency. "Okay, I'll just enjoy the ride."

"Shut up, Tyler." She leaned forward and found his mouth with her tongue, her hands stroking his face.

* * *

Afterward, they dressed quickly, almost self-consciously. They both had that same thought at the same time, then grinned at each other. Annie came over to him and kissed him on the cheek.

"Thanks for giving in to superior forces."

"My pleasure, lady."

"Mine too. Hey, I guess we'll go a little farther, then head back."

She led the way to a path that skirted the rim of a ravine. The trail wound its way down by a series of switchbacks, but from here they could survey the entire valley all the way back to Crow's Fork. They traded serious glances when they saw the dark plume of smoke twisting up from town. Annie raised her binoculars.

"Oh, my God."

"What is it?"

"I think it's O'Toole's place—at least it *was*, by the location. But there's nothing left of it except charred wood, as far as I can tell."

"Let me see." He took the binoculars and trained them on the source of the smoke. "You sure that's O'Toole's place?"

She nodded grimly. He held the binoculars and lowered his sightline to skim the valley and the trail down below their lookout point. "Hey," he said, "somebody's coming our way."

"Can you make out who?"

"Nope. Here, take a look."

She peered in the direction he was pointing, but all she could see was the upper torso of a person making his way through the tall grass and trees. All she could be sure of was that it was a man—or appeared to be.

"Maybe it's Alex," she murmured. "We better head down and meet him—whoever it is."

Ham took his concealed pistol out of its shoulder holster, checked for a full clip, released the safety, and nodded. She took him by the hand and they began the hike down from the rim into the valley. The trail varied in steepness, then

leveled to a moderate incline. If their view of the mysterious
intruder had been intermittent, it was now totally obscured
by the woods. Ham held his gun at the ready.

"Are you sure he had to come this way?"

Annie gave a half nod. "Unless he's just wandering, this
is the only real trail."

Then through the foliage, they saw the figure, very near
now. Ham held Annie by the arm and they backed off the
path behind a large tree trunk, flattening themselves out of
sight. The figure was within five yards, and they still
couldn't see his face. Ham vaulted out onto the trail, gun
aimed dead-on. "Freeze!"

"Whatever you say," Frank O'Toole answered.

Annie recognized the voice and jumped into O'Toole's
surprised arms. "Frank! You're okay!"

He pried himself out of her bear hug. "Well, I've been
better."

"You're right," she said as she looked him over. He was
smudged from head to foot with ashes and soot, his hair and
beard were singed, and he smelled like a char-broiled steak.
"We saw the fire from the ridge. Was it your place?" she
asked.

He nodded solemnly. "It's gone, Annie, in several puffs
of smoke."

"What about Maragato and Chris?" Tyler broke in.

"Maragato's dead."

"Shit," Ham said.

"He was also a Visitor in sheep's clothing."

Ham did a double take. "A friggin' Visitor? Son of a
bitch."

"Chris killed him just before the house exploded. I think
Chris got away, but I've no idea where he went to. He's a
good man. I'm sure he'll be all right on his own for a bit."

"What about Alex?" Annie asked hesitantly.

"The Visitors have him, I believe. They know that he
knows where you and Mr. Donovan are, and I think Lydia is
very determined to get that information. What we went
through is a long and involved story. Why don't we go up to
the mine and I'll tell you the whole tale. . . ."

* * *

"But how did you get away?" Donovan asked as they passed a canteen of water around. The group was seated in the shade at the mine entrance.

"Well," O'Toole continued, "the smoke was already too thick for me to see where Chris had gone to. I could hear his voice, but that was it. I could tell he was way across the room, probably near a window. But I didn't think there was any chance I could get over there. Also, I knew the fire was getting close to the propane tank, and I figured I better take the nearest exit route."

Annie nodded. "Of course—downstairs."

"Right." O'Toole noticed quizzical looks coming from Tyler and Donovan. "In the middle of the front room, there's a trapdoor leading down to a storage basement. Well, the fellow who built the house was something of a survivalist, so he put a shelter down there—concrete walls, heavy door, the whole bit. And the shelter has a tunnel that leads out of the house and comes up aboveground about thirty yards away, under cover of the woods. I got to the shelter with the flames flicking at my heels. It was a close call, I'll tell you. But from there, it was perfectly easy and simple to escape into the woods."

"The question is, what do we do now?" Annie said. "If Alex gives them the location of this mine, they'll be up here in no time."

"And if he doesn't," Donovan said, "then Lydia is going to keep killing hostages until someone turns us in—even if she kills the whole town."

"Which she'll do," O'Toole said, "since no one else knows where you are except me. And I'm obviously not there to tell her."

"We can't let that go on," Donovan said firmly, letting out a deep breath and setting his mouth in a thin line.

"What're we going to do, Gooder—waltz down there and give ourselves up?"

Donovan let the sarcastic question hang in the air for a moment as he looked from face to face. "In a word, yeah."

Ham rose to his feet, face turning red. "Are you nuts, Donovan? Have you finally lost it?"

"No, I'm not nuts, and I don't mean both of us."

"Well, if you expect *me* to saunter down to Lizard-Lips Lydia, you *are* crazy."

Donovan shook his head. "No, not you—me. You and Barry have to get this report back to L.A.—to Julie and the others before it's too late. I'm expendable—this information isn't."

"Mike," Ham began, but the tone of his voice indicated he knew Donovan was right.

"You know we don't have any choice."

"She'll kill you, Donovan," Annie protested.

"No, I don't think she will. She wants me alive, to present me to Diana. I'm too important to them to kill—at least not right away. Annie, you guide Ham and Barry out of this area. Get 'em far enough from here that they can call Barry's pilot and have a fighting chance to fly out without getting shot down by Lydia's four ships."

"Three," O'Toole corrected. "We've got some local saboteurs doing their bit to make Lydia's stay less than pleasant."

"Hmm, that's always nice to hear," Donovan said. "Ham, you were right about one thing, I think. I can't just waltz down and give Lydia a hug. We want to make this look convincing, and we want her to lay off the town. O'Toole, you're going to capture me and bring me in."

"Gee, I've always wanted to play bounty hunter," he said dryly. "I'll do it if you think it'll make a difference."

"I think it will," Donovan repeated. "But you do run a risk—some people might think less fondly of you for being a turncoat. Still want to do it?"

"If it increases the chances of Lydia getting the hell away from Crow's Fork before anyone else dies, no question about it."

Donovan stretched, cracking his knuckles nervously. "Well, okay, then. Let's saddle up and get out of here."

Barry and Annie started to move first. Tyler gave Donovan a searching look, their eyes locking.

"We'll get back and get you out, Gooder," Tyler said. "You just stay alive for a while, okay? I can't imagine life without you always giving me a hard time."

Donovan nodded. "I'll be waiting—if Lydia doesn't get impatient and kill me first."

"Use your charm. I'd give you a lesson, but we're outa time."

Chapter 15

Donovan and O'Toole paused in the woods and dismounted from their horses just before emerging into the foothills that led down to Crow's Fork. In the distance, the smoldering remains of the trail guide's house gave off a diaphanous veil of smoke.

"Are you sure you want to go through with this, Donovan?"

Donovan chuckled anxiously. "No, not at all, but I don't have much choice."

"Sure you do. You could just turn around and walk off into the sunset. I'm the only one who would know, and Lord knows, I wouldn't hold it against you."

"That's not a choice," Donovan said, shaking his head.

The big Irishman narrowed his eyes. "You act like all this is somehow your fault, and you've got to atone for the sin of bringing the Visitors down on our heads."

Donovan's expression hardened, and he looked away. "Maybe I do feel like it's my fault. I should've been smart enough to guess that Maragato might've been a Visitor posing as one of us. Maybe I should've ordered a medical checkup. Maybe—"

"Maybe's don't pay the rent, Mike."

"But they do teach lessons. Just hope I live long enough to remember this one and apply it next time." He sat down on a tree stump, resting his chin on his hands. "I don't know—I make so many mistakes. And this time, innocent people died because of one of them."

"You don't think great generals and military leaders didn't make mistakes all through history?"

"You calling me a great military leader?" Donovan asked, cutting irony in his voice.

O'Toole smiled gently. "No, but you're doing your best. All of you in the resistance are, when a lot of the rest of us aren't even pitching in. I was in Vietnam, Mike. I saw mistakes you wouldn't believe. Hell, the whole bloody war was a mistake from start to finish. And you're thinking of it the wrong way. You're not making mistakes. You're more likely just trying your damnedest to clean up after *other* people's mistakes."

"What other people?"

"People who made errors of judgment that let the Visitors get a toehold during both their invasions."

"Hey, O'Toole, it's hard to blame people when they're dealing with something like this. Jesus, I doubt that West Point spends much time teaching cadets what to do in case of alien invasions of Earth. And where are Presidents and prime ministers supposed to check for the way past leaders reacted to invasions by five-mile-wide flying saucers?"

"Thank you for making my point. If those people who're trained to be leaders and deal with world crises couldn't have been prepared for something like this, how in hell could you have been?"

"My mind says you're right, O'Toole, but my gut still tells me I should've known better." Donovan shrugged. "What the hell. Guess we better get this over with before Lydia starts rounding up more hostages."

James and a Visitor guard saw O'Toole and Donovan approaching on foot. Weapons raised, the aliens moved out to meet them. Donovan's hands were tied behind his back as O'Toole led him.

"Well, Mr. Donovan, this is a welcome turn of events. Lydia has been hoping you'd arrive."

"Yeah, I'll bet."

"We'll take him from here," James said, nodding to the guard, who shoved Donovan ahead with the tip of his laser rifle. Donovan stumbled forward, then turned and gave the alien a dirty look.

"I guess you won't be needing me for anything," O'Toole said.

"On the contrary," James answered. "I think Lydia will want to thank you personally. Come with us."

James turned and strode quickly toward the command skyfighter. He pressed a button next to the hatch and it slid open. "Commander," he said, ducking his head inside, "we have Donovan."

There was a studied moment of silence from inside, as if Lydia didn't want to appear too anxious to claim her prize. Finally she came out of the small craft, stepping down slowly, ceremoniously, then standing straight and tall. "Mr. Donovan," she said with great dignity and satisfaction. She turned to O'Toole. "I'm gratified to see you alive, Mr. O'Toole. We'd thought you'd perished when your house burned down. An unfortunate act of sabotage. Perhaps being a victim yourself convinced you the correct thing to do was in fact to find Mr. Donovan and give him to us."

"We just want you to leave Crow's Fork, Lydia. You've got what you came for."

"Not entirely," she interrupted. "I also came for Mr. Tyler. I have a feeling Mr. Donovan knows something of his friend's whereabouts."

"Not a thing, Lydia," Donovan said evenly, trying not to sound defiant. He didn't think provoking her would accomplish much at this point.

"We'll find out very soon. James, take him to the interrogation room."

Lydia's second-in-command obeyed, directing four shock troopers to the task.

"Prepare him," Lydia called after them. "I'll be right there to start the questioning. We've got no time to waste." She went back inside her skyfighter.

O'Toole walked slowly away, drifting in the direction of his burned-out house but keeping a close eye on where they were taking Donovan. The Visitors hustled him to a glass-fronted one-story building that had a sign over its door that said "CLINIC." To be sure, he waited until they actually went in. He wondered what Lydia meant by "interrogation room," and his stomach churned as he thought of the possible perversions now occurring in this place normally used to heal people.

Donovan looked around. The waiting room out front looked like the one in any other community clinic in a small town. Magazines were left open where people had thrown them when the Visitors had arrived, and toys and building blocks were strewn across the floor, discarded by children scooped up by their panicked parents.

"I'm not due for a physical for months," Donovan said to no one in particular.

They walked him through a door to what had been an examining room but was now occupied by more Visitor guards. In the center of the room, the table had been modified—a horizontal tubelike plexiglass apparatus that could encompass a body had been placed over it. Wires and electrodes entered the tube, hanging inside it, awaiting a subject to which they could be attached.

"Tanning salon?" Donovan murmured. The Visitors ignored him.

Lydia strode into the examining area, boots clicking smartly on the tile floor. "Put him in there."

Two of the guards pinioned his arms to his sides and started to lift him off his feet. He elbowed one in the face and tried to trip the other with his leg. Two other Visitors joined the scuffle and held him firmly.

"Mr. Donovan," Lydia said sharply, "resisting isn't going to accomplish anything except perhaps the breaking of some of your limbs. My guards have undergone considerable training—gentleness was not part of the curriculum."

"Wouldn't you have been disappointed if I didn't try?"

"Not in the least. Get him in there, *now*."

This time five guards swept him up and had him horizontal before he could resist. They slid him feetfirst into the clear tube. The ends were still open, and Lydia waved two technicians in. While the guards secured his hands and feet, the techs attached the wires and electrodes to his head and neck. The female technician unbuttoned his shirt and attached one pad to his chest, over his heart.

"Lydia, didn't anybody ever tell you the way to a man's heart is through his stomach?"

Placing hands on hips, she scowled. "I assume that's a human joke of some sort. Biologically, it's not very likely. Since you may be curious, that particular stimu-pad is to shock your heart back into operation in case it should stop at any point during the interrogation process."

Donovan swallowed, perspiration beading on his forehead in spite of his attempts to stay calm. "Why do I get the feeling this isn't going to be a multiple-choice test?"

"I don't want you to expire unexpectedly, Mr. Donovan. Not until I'm done with you."

"Wouldn't Diana prefer to have me alive?" The tube opening near his head was sealed and his muffled voice bounced off the surface just a few inches over his face. He hoped they could still hear him outside.

"I suppose she would," Lydia said. "But Diana's wishes aren't my prime concern. My questioning will get all the vital information possible from that brain of yours. Diana could question you from now until doomsday, as you humans might say, and she'd learn no more than I would. Maybe even less. I think she'd prefer you and Tyler dead together, than you alive alone."

"Gee, Ham would be thrilled to hear that. I know he's always considered us a team," Donovan joked.

"Ready, Commander," said the female technician.

"Good," Lydia said. "Intensity one—"

The female tech had moved to a control panel containing what looked to Donovan like EKG and brain-wave monitors. The tech threw four toggle switches and Donovan felt a tingling course over his skin, like a troop of tiny ants marching across his body. It wasn't at all unpleasant, almost a gentle tickling. But he tensed himself, knowing that it wasn't intended to be painful. He guessed it simply meant the device was activated, the current barely running into him. He felt light-headed at the same time, as if the electrodes attached to his head were drawing energy away from his brain. The room began to spin and a wave of nausea wobbled through his gut.

"All right, Mr. Donovan," Lydia said, her voice echoing from far away. "Tell me where Mr. Tyler is."

"Planet Earth," came Donovan's reply. Disconcertingly, his mouth moved slowly, his voice sounding to his ears as if it came through a two-second-tape-delay mechanism.

From his prone position, he couldn't see Lydia nod to the female technician at the console. But the current exploded through Donovan's body and seared every nerve ending. He couldn't stop the scream that leaped from his throat involuntarily. When it was over, he twitched for four or five seconds like a fish flopping on a boat deck.

"That was just a short dose, Mr. Donovan," Lydia said. Her voice came from a speaker embedded in the plexiglass at his left ear. "The more you refuse to answer, the less pleasant the experience will become. And I should warn you, there's not much tissue damage from this technique, so you won't easily die from what we're doing to you, not until the highest settings. You may lose consciousness, but when you come to, the pain will still be there. Please consider that for a moment."

"Thanks for the advice."

"I see your sense of humor hasn't been diminished by the pain. Perhaps longer-duration suffering will have some effect. Now, think very hard, Donovan. Your continued good health may depend on your answer. Where can I find Ham Tyler?"

Donovan tried to shrug, and his face twitched into a semblance of a smile. "The thing is, Lydia, I really don't know."

The security cadré commander turned to the life-monitor technician. "Analysis, Margaret?"

The technician pursed her lips as she examined a repeat reading of Donovan's physiological response. "Inconclusive, Commander. I think he knows more than he's telling but is being truthful when he says he doesn't know Tyler's location. I suggest trying another line of questioning while he's still conscious."

"Very well. Donovan, have you been receiving smuggled weapons from other resistance groups?"

"No."

Without warning, Lydia angrily reached over to Margaret's console and twisted the control. Donovan screamed in surprised agony and the technician quickly turned the dial back to minimum, then gave her superior officer a harsh look. "Commander, let me do my job. There *is* some danger of—"

"I don't care," Lydia snapped. "I want answers from this human, and pain can be a very convincing prod."

"*Not* if you kill him," Margaret said icily.

Lydia narrowed her eyes and spoke in a quiet, intense voice. "I thought you said he could be revived—"

"Under controlled circumstances. But if enough power is applied in too rapid a surge, there will be nothing to revive, Commander. It wouldn't be easy to kill him, but it is *possible*. I'm trained in the use of this equipment. With all due respect, you're not."

Donovan's eyes were blurred by tears. He was paralyzed, completely numbed by the last jolt. He felt suspended in a vast ocean of nothingness, empty space that somehow supported him—no, *trapped* him in its center—unable to move or drift or float in a direction he might want to choose. His body was more a part of that void than a part of him.

He saw a form approach his cage, a hand pound on it. He'd heard faraway voices but couldn't make out what they were saying. But now he heard, loud and clear, Lydia saying, "Donovan, tell me what I want to know. Answer these questions or you'll die painfully and slowly. I promise."

His vision cleared and he saw Lydia above him, caressing his plexiglass cocoon, her voice suddenly gentle.

"I know you think you're protecting your friends, Donovan. And I know some of those friends are Visitors, members of what you call the fifth column. Has it occurred to you some of them are not your friends, but my spies? How do you know the information they pass along to you is real? How do you know they're not passing along *dis*infor-

mation to you, designed to lead you in exactly the direction
I want you to go?"

Donovan tried to speak, tried to protest. His lips fluttered
helplessly, muscles and nerves still unable to respond. All
he could form was the word "*No*."

Lydia smiled down at him, her face distorted by the
curvature of the enclosure. "Oh, yes, yes, Donovan. I'm
afraid it's true. Would you like an example? The secret plan
you probably know about now, brought to you by one of my
trusted aides, Barry—the one to invade the United States by
disrupting power? It's a fake, a planted strategy to mislead
you and lure you out of hiding at a time and place I'd know
about. After you and your band of criminals stole my
prisoners, I genuinely wanted to repay you for your
kindness. You might say I'm just beginning."

Donovan's mind reeled, tumbled, and fell down some
black abyss. The Visitor's voice echoed, growing distant,
fading to nothing. . . .

"Revive him," Lydia ordered. "Increase power for the
next treatment."

"He needs some recovery time," Margaret said. "If he
doesn't have it, he could die the next time he loses
consciousness."

"I don't care—I want answers and I want them immediately."

"You won't get answers from a dead human," Margaret
shot back.

"Follow your orders or you'll be replaced, Lieutenant."

Margaret clenched her jaw. "Yes—*Commander*."

"It's time to make a move," Julie said to the small group
of resistance members gathered in Club Creole's downstairs
hideaway.

"I'm with you," Kyle Bates said eagerly. He stood
behind Elizabeth, resting a hand on her shoulder.

"Fine," said Maggie Blodgett, brushing a wisp of honey-
blond hair off her cheek. "But make a move where and
how?"

"Julie," Willie said gently. "I know how important it is
for us to get Mike and Ham back safely, but without

knowing what we're up against, would not it be like spitting
under the wind?"

"*In*to the wind, Willie," Maggie said, patting him on the
arm. She was several inches taller than the little Visitor, and
she smiled down at him.

"Doesn't matter," Kyle insisted. "We have to do
something."

Julie raised a hand, asking for quiet. "Look, everything
this bunch does is voluntary. This mission is my idea, my
responsibility. Anyone who disagrees with my decision to
go ahead with it isn't bound to be a part of it."

"Hey, it's not that, Julie," Maggie said. "It's just that
personal feelings have to be kept in check."

Julie turned sharply. "Is that what you think this is, some
brave gesture on my part to save Mike?"

"Julie, I've been there," Maggie said softly. "Remember, I had to leave Brad behind when we blew up that water-
treatment plant during the first invasion. Nobody can totally
block out feelings—we're only human. Sorry, Willie."

"That's all right, Maggie. I had the same feelings for
Harmony when she—she died on the Mother Ship."

"Hey, I don't want to interrupt this encounter session,"
Kyle said, "but we've gotta make some decisions."

"Kyle's right—and so are you, Maggie," Julie said.
"I'm aware of my feelings. They may be part of why I want
to do something, but they're not clouding my judgment. If
any of you think they are, I trust you to tell me. I also trust
you to listen to me if I can convince you that's not the
case." Julie paused and looked around. "Anybody seen
Elias?"

Before anyone could answer, they heard footsteps from
the secret passageway leading down to the old speakeasy
from the street above. The door panel slid open and Elias
came in—with the young alien Zachary.

"We got us a visitor—so to speak," Elias announced.
"And we didn't even hit him upside his head this time."

Zachary gave them an uneasy smile. He'd always envied
Barry and some of the other fifth columnists. They were so
relaxed around humans. But they'd had much more expo-
sure to them. He was annoyed with himself that he couldn't

shake the feeling of being with *aliens*. Intellectually, he knew these resistance fighters would never harm him, not without reason. But it was hard to forget all the propaganda that had been used by Diana on the crews of the Visitor fleet, enforcing over and over how treacherous humans were, how they were an implacable enemy prone to barbarous acts of terror and butchery against Visitors taken prisoner. Zach had heard all that, seen the tapes—which he later learned were created by Diana's production team— showing the camps where captured Visitors were taken, the torture devices used on them, the victims of those devices. He'd been thoroughly exposed before he'd ever actually spoken to a human on this reinvasion of Earth. Like most Visitor technicians, he'd stayed aboard the Mother Ship on the initial mission, when he and his fellow crewmen had been indoctrinated to think of humans as lower life forms to be harvested for food. And that was the only condition in which he'd seen a human on that first voyage to Earth, inside food storage pods in the ship's great cryogenic holds.

"Not so bad once you get used to them," was the way Barry had put it, adding, "Don't forget, they have to look like this for their entire lives. Maybe it explains some of the way they behave. But on the whole, they're not a bad species."

"What brings you back?" Julie said now.

He held out his copy of the cassette containing Barry's report to Lydia. "This."

He went on to show them the whole plan on his holo-reader, and explained Barry's fears leading him to entrust someone else with a duplicate. "It seems his fears were well-founded," he said sadly. "If you haven't heard from your team and Barry hasn't been able to return to the Mother Ship—"

"Don't say it," Elias interrupted. "We all feel bad enough without going over and over it. We gotta do something positive, man."

"Like what?" Willie asked.

"Like take a trip up north and see what's been happening," Julie said. "We know the coordinates of where they were all supposed to meet."

"But we can't get there," Kyle said.

"Not all the way up to the mine, maybe," Elias countered, "but we *can* get as far as that dinky little town—what's it called?"

"Crow's Fork," Julie said. "And we *can* get up to that mine. We can use Zach's transportation."

"Hey, man, that's right!" Elias said. "We got wings!"

"Uh, Elias," Willie said softly, "skyfighters don't have wings."

"It's an expression, Willie, just an expression," Elias said happily, tweaking the Visitor's cheek. His mood was lifting for the first time in what seemed like a century.

Julie rubbed her hands together. "This is good, very good," she said almost to herself. "Not only can we make great time, but we'll have some firepower too—Nathan Bates or no Nathan Bates. Okay, everybody, let's go!" The group of more than a dozen began to rise as one entity. Julie stopped and two of them bumped into her. "Hold on—we can't all go. We need some people to hold down the fort in case we hear from Tyler and Donovan, or in case anything else goes wrong. Let's see. Kyle, you and Elizabeth stay here. Um, Elias, Willie, you come with me and Zach. . . ." She continued splitting them up, taking eight along for the trip to Crow's Fork, including Maggie to pilot the skyfighter. Willie assured Zachary that she was as good as any pilot in the fleet. And they loaded their most powerful firearms. Julie hoped they wouldn't need to fight, but if the situation came up, she wanted to be ready. "Everyone in Visitor uniforms," she ordered.

As they hurried through the passageway out of Club Creole, Elias stopped Julie. "Hey, what are we gonna do when we get there?"

"How am I supposed to know? We'll do what we always do—improvise the best damned tap dance we can think of!"

Chapter 16

Alone in the town clinic, now the interrogation station, Lydia looked down at the unconscious form of Mike Donovan. His face twitched in pain every few seconds while hers remained impassive.

"Why do you humans insist on fighting us?" she said quietly. "When will it occur to you that resistance is futile. Power will prevail—that's the rule of the universe, yet you ignore it. I'd rather do this without inflicting pain, but you're not giving me any choice."

Donovan's eyelids fluttered open and Lydia sucked her breath in, caught off guard for a moment.

"You've got a choice," Donovan mumbled through cracked and dry lips. "You can leave. This is *our* planet, and we'll all die before we just hand it over to you and walk into your frozen-food holds."

"You weren't supposed it hear what I said."

"Yeah"—Donovan swallowed, wincing—"well, I did, Lydia. Why are you doing this? I know why Diana's doing it. She's power hungry and probably psychotic too, by our standards anyway. But I think you're different."

"Make no mistake, Mr. Donovan," she said coldly. "I'm just as dedicated to this mission as Diana. There's nothing—"

"Bull," Donovan whispered. "You're dedicated to protecting your own turf, grabbing more of it if you can. But you're not dedicated to killing four billion people on this planet just to satisfy the personal vanity of that great leader of yours nine light-years away from here. *He's* not the one risking his neck—*you* are, lady." He peered up at her through the plexiglass and thought he caught the barest tug of doubt at the corner of her mouth.

"We're here on a mission of survival, Donovan," Lydia answered harshly. "Nothing can get in the way of that. Are you going to argue that your people wouldn't do the same if your existence was at stake?"

He tried to shrug, but the restraints on his arms and shoulders kept him pinned down to the examining table. "I don't know, Lydia. Maybe we would. But we'd look for another way first. I don't think you have. I think your great leader cooked up this scheme, probably to make you all forget about the lousy job he's done, and you all believe every word he tells you. Don't you ever question anything?" He paused. "Besides, our existence *is* at stake. That's why we're fighting."

"You're very smug for a member of a race very near to being exterminated."

"What the hell's the difference?" he asked. "If we're going to lose, we're going to lose. But I don't have to help that ending come along. We both know damn well if we humans wind up winning again, it'll be because enough of you Visitors realized your leaders are wrong—that you've been doing *their* dirty work just to save *their* lizard hides."

"What makes you such an expert on Visitor psyches?"

Donovan shook his head. "If that surprises you, you're not as observant as you think. All the time you've been learning about us, we've been learning about you too. I've gotta say it's surprised *me* a little, but intelligent beings just don't seem to be that different. At least Visitors and humans aren't. We've had plenty of instances in our history of bad leaders grabbing power, fooling people into following them. But sooner or later the lies come out, the tides turn." Donovan's throat gave way and a racking cough shook his body.

Lydia avoided looking at his face as she tipped a bottle attached to the interrogation cage and water flowed down to a tube near Donovan's mouth. "Drink it," she said neutrally.

He narrowed his eyes at her for a second, trying to figure out if this was really an act of kindness or if he was reading things into Lydia's response. It didn't matter, he decided, and angled the tube into his parched mouth and gulped the cool water.

Four Visitor guards entered the room, forcibly escorting Frank O'Toole, his hands bound behind him.

"Get him ready," Lydia ordered the guards.

Margaret led four technicians in from a side area, wheeling in two more of the tube-shaped confinement devices. One was empty—Donovan presumed that was for O'Toole—but he was surprised to see Alex inside the other, sealed in with the electrodes and sensors already attached to his body.

Pale and shaken, O'Toole looked around. Donovan waved weakly at him, but Alex lay on the table without moving. Blood trickled from his nose and the corner of his mouth. The young guide's face was bruised and his clothing tattered as if he'd been severely beaten before being brought here.

"Why are you doing this?" O'Toole said to Lydia, his voice a hoarse whisper.

"Because I need information and I need it now. You and your young friend, Alex, are more expendable than Donovan, so you're going to be questioned before him. As you can see, Alex has been rather badly treated. I am sorry about that, but he evidently provoked some of my guards into losing their tempers. Now I'm going to let you watch what he goes through. If he's foolish and refuses to tell me what I want to know, you'll be next. I do hope, if it comes to that, that simply observing the interrogation of Alex will be enough to convince you to be less stubborn, Mr. O'Toole. I warn you, my patience is growing very thin."

The security commander nodded to Margaret, who threw the series of switches on her console to start the machines. O'Toole looked on as Alex's body tensed involuntarily. The young man seemed to be beyond conscious behavior. O'Toole felt a queasiness welling up in his stomach, and he glanced quickly around the room for a basin, just in case he had to vomit. A guard stood ready at either side of him to prevent him from escaping, but for the time being, they let him stand free.

Lydia moved around Alex's clear cocoon, like a cat circling prey that wasn't quite disabled. "The pain grows worse, doesn't it, Alex? You can make it stop, make it go away. All you have to do is answer the questions."

Donovan tried to lift his head. From his prone position in the isolation tube, he could barely hear the Visitor commander's voice from across the small room, but he couldn't make out exactly what was happening.

"Where can I find Ham Tyler?" Lydia asked soothingly.

"Don't know. . . ."

O'Toole swallowed hard at the sound of Alex's voice—thin as a thread, distant as if coming from the bottom of a well. He shifted his eyes to the guards—they'd edged a half step closer to him, prepared to move if necessary.

Lydia continued to prowl, crouching so that Alex could see her face. "Maybe you're telling me the truth, maybe you don't know where Tyler is now. Is that right, Alex?"

"Y-Yes . . . don't know now. . . ." he whimpered.

"That's a good boy. Your reward for telling the truth is no more pain. Isn't that good?"

The trail guide smiled through puffy lips. "Good."

"I'm your friend, Alex. You know that, don't you?"

"Friend? No. . . ."

Lydia frowned. "Yes, yes I am. I want to stop the hurting. I keep telling you how to do that, but you won't listen to me. Please listen to me, Alex."

His head nodded almost imperceptibly. "Y-Yes . . . listen."

"Good. Now tell me where Tyler was the last time you saw him."

"No—n-n-no. Can't tell. Swore not—"

Pressing her lips together angrily, Lydia looked over at Margaret. "Now—do it."

Margaret's mouth curled defiantly as her hand poised over the augmentation control. "He's weak—life functions barely register."

"Do it," Lydia repeated sharply.

The technician's hand turned. Alex's body arched up, but the only sound he could make was a keening echo.

Alex's cry, soft as it was, sliced into O'Toole's gut. He felt his stomach heave. *I have to do something*, he thought, and he started forward. Instantly, two impossibly strong hands clamped onto his upper arms, squeezing with enough pressure to make him yelp. He could imagine they would be able to snap bones if they chose to. They lifted him off the floor and placed him back down hard where he'd started from.

Ignoring everyone else in the room, Lydia now draped herself over the tube, glaring down directly into Alex's face, her words coming with a guttural intensity. "Time is running out, time is almost gone—your time, your *life*. Talk now or you'll lose your chance, lose your life. Tell me where Ham Tyler is. Tell me—tell me—*tell me!*"

She looked back at Margaret. "Full power," she hissed.

The technician obeyed and O'Toole braced himself. Alex's torso twisted, his breathing came in short rasps, and then his whole body jittered in its restraint straps. The face contorted in a silent scream, and O'Toole wanted to look away but couldn't, riveted by his own horror and fear.

That'll be me.

And then Alex was still, stiffly frozen in an arched-back position, a mannequin in some madman's window advertising torture. A soft, steady tone emanated from the tech's console.

"That's it," Margaret said. "This human is dead—no chance of revival. All autonomic neuromuscular substance destroyed."

Lydia straightened. "Get rid of him." Then she turned to face O'Toole. "You see the result of prolonged interrogation. I sincerely hope you decide to cooperate quickly. Put him in."

Donovan watched helplessly as the hulking guards lifted O'Toole off his feet and inserted him into the third glass chamber.

* * *

"We haven't covered much territory," Ham Tyler said as he, Annie, and the Visitor, Barry, stopped to rest in a shady spot. They'd left the other horses at the mine.

"More than you think, Tyler," Annie said.

"Far enough to call my pilot to pick us up?" Barry asked.

"Well, that's the big question, ain't it?" Ham said. "That's something we're just not going to know for sure until we try it."

"We're heading east," Annie said, drawing a line in the dirt with a twig. "Lydia and her skyfighters are west of us. If we arrange to meet Barry's ship even farther east of here, we should have a pretty good chance of its getting there without being spotted."

Tyler licked his lips, then took a swig from his canteen. "Pretty good chance may not be enough, Halsey."

"It'll have to be when it's the only chance we got, Tyler. We can't get very far on foot. And what worries me is, the longer Donovan and O'Toole are in Lydia's hands, the more chance she's gonna have of breaking 'em and getting 'em to talk about where we went. So we face a future of diminishing returns, if you get my drift."

Ham nodded. "Okay. Good point." He nodded to Barry, and the Visitor took his communicator out of a pocket.

"Teri, this is Barry. Come in, please."

"Yes, Captain," the pilot replied after a second or two.

"We think it's time. One of the humans with me will give you the coordinates where you should meet us. Are you ready to record?"

"Yes, sir. But aren't you where you were before?"

"No," Barry answered. "We had to move. When you take off, fly as low as possible. We don't know what Lydia is doing or whether she knows we're out here. We don't know whether she'll be looking for another skyfighter. Proceed as if you *are* being hunted. Understood?"

"Understood," Teri said. "What if I'm spotted?"

Tyler grabbed the communicator from Barry. "If you're spotted, forget about us. Get the hell away from us and don't come back." He handed the transmitter back to the alien.

"Who was that?" Teri asked.

"Follow those instructions," Barry said. He turned to Annie. "Ready?"

She nodded and spoke into the communicator. "Okay now, I'm also going to describe the terrain and give you some landmarks to look for. . . ."

Perhaps twelve years old, the child watched the Crow's Fork clinic building from the woods behind it. With mocha skin, eyes that were nearly black, and curly dark hair, the slim child could have passed for a boy or a girl. The name on her blue sweat shirt, "Jacqueline," stitched in script across the chest, was the only certain giveaway.

She stood lightly on her toes, unafraid but with the tension of a doe ready to flee at the first inkling of danger. From her hidden vantage point, she saw the Visitor second-in-command, James, walk swiftly from Lydia's skyfighter to the clinic.

Jacqueline skipped gracefully over a fallen tree and disappeared into the woods.

Lydia stepped back from the tube containing Frank O'Toole just as James entered the interrogation area.

"Is this one still alive?" he asked.

The commander nodded. "Occasionally, the demonstration has the desired effect. It didn't take long for O'Toole to become cooperative."

James raised his eyebrows. "You found out where Tyler is?"

"More or less. I think we have enough information to find him along with the fifth-column traitor. Was there something you wanted to tell me?"

"Yes, Lydia, and it may be tied in to what you've found out from O'Toole. We've picked up readings on one of our skyfighters. There's an unauthorized presence in this zone."

"Oh?"

"It was flying extremely low in the mountains nearby—dangerously low, in fact, as if the pilot was trying to avoid detection."

* * *

"Okay, light it." Chris Faber held the crossbow at arm's length. The tip of the arrow was covered with a small glass container, a cloth wick coming out and wrapping around the shaft. "I gotta tell you, I never shot a Molotov cocktail arrow before."

Hank, the blond teenager, held a long fireplace match, ready to strike it. "Darned clever, these teen terrorists," he said.

"It won't go far, but it should get the job done. And what's in that bottle should be enough to do quite a lot of damage," said Bradley, the shorter kid. "But don't light it until Chris is ready to actually shoot it. If it works like it's supposed to, and it goes off before we want it to, we're gonna look like three charcoal briquettes."

Chris turned carefully and aimed over a hedge separating their location from the parking area where the three remaining Visitor skyfighters squatted, waiting.

"You set?" Bradley asked.

"Yeah." The bow steadied in Chris's grip.

"Okay," Bradley said, "light it, Hank."

Hank scraped the match head on the tree next to him. The tip flared, and he gingerly touched it to the wick. As soon as he drew the match away, Chris released the trigger. The arrow arced high, wobbling because of the odd aerodynamics of its modified point, and landed squarely atop the skyfighter nearest the woods. A split second later, it exploded, spewing liquid flame over the craft's roof, spilling down into the open side hatch. The Visitor guards reacted, but it was too late to do much except watch another vehicle catch fire.

"Okay, boys, let's get the hell out of here," Chris said, turning swiftly and nearly trampling Jacqueline as she stood right in his path. "Jesus, kid, I coulda killed you!"

"Jacqueline," Bradley said peevishly, "I know you like to sneak up on people, but one of these days—"

"I know where they're keeping your friends," she said sweetly. "In the clinic."

Chris shook his head. "Leave it to the lizards to turn a

doc's office into a chamber of horrors. Good work, kid," he said, reaching out to shake the little girl's hand. "That's our next target."

"How do we hit it?" Hank asked.

Chris led them back into the safety of the woods. "Let's give that a little thought."

Lydia and James left Donovan and O'Toole under guard and under glass in the interrogation room and headed for the front door of the clinic, then stopped short one step outside when they saw the fire and smoke across the center of town.

James felt his knees weaken, and he winced in anticipation of Lydia's reaction.

"That's wonderful—we're down to two ships," she said in a low growl. "That means we either send only one to go against this mysterious vessel you spotted, or we send both and have no backups here in case anything should happen to both ships in combat."

"Lydia, the odds of one skyfighter taking out two are—"

She silenced him with an unblinking glare. "What were the odds of a small town under our control destroying one land rover and two air vehicles? We'll send both ships up because we have no choice. We have to stop this unauthorized vessel no matter what it's doing here. Get both flight crews ready, and post guards here at the interrogation clinic."

Chris peered through binoculars at the flurry of activity down in the town. Almost all the Visitor shock troopers clambered aboard the two skyfighters. Several struggled to put out the blazing ship nearby, and a handful stood watch outside the clinic.

"So what's the plan?" Bradley asked.

"Oh, a little high tech, a little low tech," Chris said. "You guys know how to make a stink bomb?"

Hank laughed. "Hell, yeah."

Chris nodded. "Good. That's the low tech."

"What's the high tech?" Bradley wanted to know.

"A bluff."

All three kids said in unison, "Huh?"

Before Chris could answer, they were distracted by the whispering of the Visitor skyfighters as their antigrav propulsion systems fired up and their hatches closed. Kicking up dust and dirt from the road and lawn where they'd rested, the duckbilled aircraft lifted off and banked steeply toward the east.

"Where do you think they're going?" Hank said.

"Don't know," Chris replied. "But wherever it is, they're in a mighty big hurry."

"Good break for us," Bradley said. "There were thirty Visitor soldiers to begin with. Three were killed when we blew up the first skyfighter. Twenty-two went up in the last two ships—that leaves five guarding the clinic."

"Pretty good odds," Jacqueline piped up. "Four of us against five of them."

Bradley turned sharply. "You're not going, Jackie."

"Why not?" she demanded, twisting her face into an angry frown.

"Because you're not big enough," Bradley shot back.

"That's stupid," she said, drawing herself up to her full height, barely up to Chris's hip. "It's 'cause I'm a girl."

Bradley rolled his eyes. "It is not—"

"Sexist," she said, biting off the word.

Chris put a fatherly arm around her thin shoulders and drew her a few feet away. "Don't let it get to you, kid," he said softly. "You can do things they can't, like sneakin' through the woods. You're too valuable to waste on somethin' like this. Besides, someday you're gonna be running this whole operation."

"Well, okay," she said a bit sullenly. "But I'm going to hold you to that."

Chapter 17

As the two skyfighters flew east, Lydia, in one of them, watched the ground scanner while James kept his eyes on the air-to-air sensors. Their targets—Tyler's party on the ground and the rogue fighter in the sky—continued to elude them.

"How much longer do we search?" James asked.

"I'm in no hurry," the commander answered. "We search until we've covered all possible nearby territory. And if we lose Mr. Tyler, we still have a prize to present to Diana. Michael Donovan is quite securely in our hands."

"I'd feel better if we'd left more guards there, Lydia."

"We couldn't—we don't know if this stolen fighter is carrying armed rebels. We can't risk being overwhelmed by a force outnumbering our own."

Donovan flexed his fingers. He was still under the plexiglass interrogation device, and the muscles in his fingers were about the only ones he could move. It was starting to get warm in his tube. They'd opened the end at his feet, but body heat was collecting faster than it could be vented out. Across the room, O'Toole was still on his back inside the clear cocoon, but he stirred enough to convince Donovan he'd survived his own interrogation without too much damage.

Whatever O'Toole had told Lydia, the Visitors certainly had found it interesting. Donovan hadn't been able to hear clearly, but he was fairly certain Lydia had tortured some pretty vital information out of the Irishman. And if that was true, he was equally sure O'Toole would be blaming himself for being too weak to die the way Alex had, without giving anything away. Donovan hoped O'Toole would be able to recall some of the pep talk he'd given when Donovan had been holding himself responsible for the whole situation that had developed at Crow's Fork.

What if they'd done it to me again? Donovan thought. He'd place no bets that he would've been able to withstand another session—not after seeing what they'd done to Alex.

And was it guts or stubbornness that gave the young guide the strength to resist? Donovan had no idea, but whatever it was, it sure had been a surprise. Maybe Alex had decided he had something to prove after nearly becoming a turncoat at the outset.

I go my whole life never having to face that moment of truth, Donovan mused, *never having to make a choice between betrayal and death. Oh, my life's been in danger from time to time, but only because I put myself and my stupid minicam in front of all sorts of things that can kill me, like Salvadoran death squads and helicopter gunships, crazy snipers, bank robbers caught in the act. But I never thought of those situations as really dangerous. All I was doing was getting the best damn pictures for the evening news. Now, since the Visitors have been here, I've been in spots like this at least a half dozen times. And each time, somehow I get out of it before I have to actually make that choice—give up my life or give away my friends. So I still don't know what I'd do if it really came down to it.*

And if I did talk, how would I feel? If we get out of this, what do I say to O'Toole?

He wished they could talk about it now, but the three guards in the room with them precluded any conversation. And the plexiglass cells probably muffled sound too effectively to chat through. Three guards here. Were there others outside? Maybe. And where had Lydia and James gone in such a hurry?

Donovan's mental meanderings were interrupted by the distant sound of crashing glass. Though all sounds were

distant from inside his tube, the immediate actions of the
Visitor guards told him this disruption was right here in the
room. He turned his head as much as possible in both
directions, then up and back as an odor of rotten eggs
seeped in through the opening near his toes, making him
gag.

*Shit, I get through the torture and I'm gonna suffocate in
here because of a stink bomb!*

There was a second crash—through another window, he
assumed. Someone was bombarding the clinic! Despite the
smell making him progressively more nauseous, Donovan
grinned to himself. Someone knew he was here, and they
were trying to get him out.

But with a stink bomb?

The guards covered their mouths and scurried to the
broken windows, searching for the source of the attack.
Curls of acrid smoke twisted toward the ceiling, and the
Visitors finally had to back out to escape the sensory
onslaught.

Four coughing aliens stumbled out the front door of the
clinic building as one more smashed through the big plate-
glass window. They all tore their helmets off and sucked in
huge breaths of outside air, their unprotected eyes squinting
into the midday sun.

"Freeze—don't move," said Chris Faber.

The Visitors looked up to see Chris, Hank, and Bradley
pointing guns at them. The lieutenant in command of the
detail started to go for his laser rifle on the ground at his feet
where he'd dropped it.

"Don't touch it," Chris said evenly. "We got armor-
piercing bullets that'll rip your arms off. Also got a little red
toxin dust if you need more convincing." He held up a
small vial.

The alien thought better of it and remained standing still.

"Hands over your heads. Clasp 'em on top," Chris
ordered. "That's right. Now, this young fella is gonna come
over and relieve you of any weapons you got weighing you
down. Don't move and maybe you'll live to have grand-
lizards. Move a muscle and you'll all be buzzard meat." He

nodded to Hank, who gulped nervously and then moved toward the shock troopers. He tossed the big laser rifles and smaller sidearms over to Chris, who lined them up with his feet.

"Thank you, gentlemen," Chris said. "Okay, Bradley, where's this cellar you said'll hold these jokers?"

"Right this way."

"Jackie," Chris called.

The little black girl appeared from the woods behind the clinic. "Yeah, Chris?" She held a canvas backpack in one hand.

"Put on that gas mask and go in and see if Donovan and O'Toole are okay. If they are, cut 'em loose. They'll know what to do with these guns here. Tell 'em we'll be back soon's we get these fellas bedded down for the afternoon." He reached down and scooped up one Visitor rifle and one hand laser. "Okay, boys, nap time," he said, gesturing with the rifle barrel.

Jacqueline watched them go for a moment, then reached into her pack like a schoolgirl digging through a purse. The filter mask was decidedly different from the items she usually carried around, but she slipped it over her head and tightened up the straps like a combat veteran, then turned and marched into the smoky clinic.

She followed the soft sound of coughing into the back examining area. Donovan and O'Toole were shaking their glass cages as the fumes swirled around them. The girl pressed her masked face up against Donovan's tube, and his coughing skipped a beat. His eyes bugged open in amazement. "What the hell are you?"

Jacqueline didn't bother to reply. She simply ran her hands along the underside of the tube and found some latches—three of them. She snapped each one open and the top lifted like a canopy. Then she released the restraints on Donovan's arms, wrists, and ankles.

Chest heaving, Donovan half rolled, half fell from the examining table, and pitched himself out the door, through the waiting room, and didn't stop until he slumped to his knees outside the building. Gradually, the paroxysm of coughing eased back to a wheeze. Only then did Donovan notice that O'Toole had joined him on hands and knees in the dirt and gravel.

The elfin being in the gas mask stood watching them. "Are you all right?" it said in a gauzy voice, through the filters.

Donovan swallowed three times to make sure he had control of his throat again. "Yeah, thanks. Now—who and what *are* you?"

An eerie giggle came through the mask and the creature pulled it off, then smiled at them.

"Little girl," O'Toole said hoarsely, "where are the Visitors?"

"O'Toole," Donovan said, "we're evidently not the only ones wondering about that." He glanced along the street.

Timidly, the people of Crow's Fork began peeking out open doors and venturing onto porches.

Donovan straightened up.

"You're supposed to know what to do with these," said Jacqueline. She pointed at the pile of alien weapons a few yards away.

Donovan's mouth fell open. "Oh my God! Where did you get these? If my mouth wasn't dryer than Death Valley, I'd start salivating! O'Toole, *look* at these!" He turned to the girl again. "Where'd they come from?"

"*They* got them from the Visitor guards," she said, pointing down the street.

Donovan followed her finger and saw Chris and two teenaged boys coming toward him. "Boy, are you a sight for sore eyes."

Chris grinned broadly. "Glad to see you're in one piece."

"You wanna tell us what's going on here? What're you running, a children's crusade?"

"You watch who you're calling children," Bradley snarled, brandishing his rifle menacingly.

Chris chuckled. "Don't worry, Donovan. It ain't loaded. Good thing the Visitors didn't try anything. Once we smoked 'em out of there, the only thing we had to hold 'em with was two bullets in my forty-five, a lot of balls, and a vial of red talcum powder."

"It's also a good thing," O'Toole said, "that Visitor olfactory nerves are just as sensitive to sulfur dioxide as ours are." He gave a residual cough.

Chris shrugged. "It was worth the guess, wasn't it? Come on and I'll show you our little prison camp, and tell you what's been goin' down while you guys have been outa circulation." They collected the weapons cache and Chris continued, "Lydia may be coming back, and if she does, she's gonna be one mighty pissed-off lizard when she finds you and her guards aren't there anymore."

"There!" James called out suddenly. He pointed to the sensor screen, narrowing down the grid pattern to center the blip that represented the mystery Visitor ship that didn't belong here.

"Channel coordinates to navigation computer," Lydia ordered.

James touched three buttons and the coordinates simultaneously flashed on the sensor screen and fed into the guidance system. The pilot, a dark-skinned male, heeled the skyfighter over to the right in a rapid maneuver.

"Closing, Commander," he said.

Lydia reached for the communications console. "This is Lydia," she said in an authoritative voice. "Priority One message to unidentified skyfighter. State your mission. Repeat—transmit authorization code and mission profile immediately."

She leaned back and waited a few seconds. James raised an eyebrow. "Doesn't look like they plan to answer," he said.

"That was their only chance. Change course to intercept." She switched comm channels. "Command One to Command Two. Follow our course. Tie into this vessel's navigation system. Combat alert. Repeat—go to combat alert. Lydia out."

Determination hardening her features, she slid out of the seat and moved to the tail gunner's compartment. The shock troopers squeezed together in the cramped cabin to let her pass. "James," she called, "you take the front weapons."

He smiled. "Yes, Commander."

The pair of skyfighters closed doggedly on the lone ship as it flew a desperate ground-hugging course. Teri was alone and had no way of firing behind her. Her only guns faced forward, and she knew they'd be of little use with two fully manned vessels approaching from the rear. Her only hope was to keep them from getting a clear shot at her—that, or surrendering. If she gave up, she'd be executed anyway, though not until Lydia and Diana had had their chances to question her. Not a pleasant prospect at all, she decided.

She knew with very little extra thought that she'd rather die here, at the controls of her ship, than in the Mother Ship's dreaded interrogation center.

Lydia's skyfighters were within visual range of the rogue ship, which still hadn't returned any message. The pursuers broke formation and swung out in two semicircles, forming a pincer as they approached from either side of Teri's ship.

Teri watched the maneuver on her screen. "Damn, they're trying to bracket me," she mumbled. From here on, she would have to rely on instinct. No time to think about things. With a deft hand, she dove at a frightening angle. As the other two ships were just completing their turns back toward her previous position, Teri saw her only chance.

She turned sharply and aimed the nose of her fighter nearly straight up, directly toward the enemy ship on her left. She would have to forget about the second ship for the moment, and hope.

Her fingers squeezed the trigger and her ship loosed a blaze of laser bolts in a continuous stream.

Her target swerved in a rapid evasive dive.

She'd missed completely. And the other ship was right behind her now. A mountain was directly in front of her, its peak higher than her present altitude. The mountain had a distinctive notch on its right face. Was this the one that

Annie had told her about, where some artist had begun carving out a monstrous sculpture, leaving it for his sons to complete after his death? If it was—

No time to go anywhere else, she thought. *If I'm wrong, I'm dead anyway. If I'm right—*

She jerked the nose of her ship up, rising, aiming over the mountain, skimming its top crags. Blue sky filled her front windows. She had to fly by sight, by feel now. Her only advantage was the little she knew about the terrain, which was more than her hunters knew. Even before she cleared the rocky crest, she kicked her skyfighter hard over to the right, and whispered a quick prayer.

Behind her, the pursuing ship did the same thing—an instant too late, for just over this peak was a second, slightly taller mountain. Teri's blind advance maneuver allowed her to skirt the sheer face of the second, but the other fighter had made its move too slowly and it glanced off the cliffs, cartwheeled crazily, and plummeted to the ground a thousand feet below. Teri heard the distant thunder of the explosion.

Lydia twisted in the gunner's nest, watching the last of her fleet of escort fighters disintegrate in a billow of angry red flame. The bulbous fireball quickly darkened as black smoke swirled around it. She clutched the mouthpiece of her headset. "I want that ship," she hissed.

The dark-skinned pilot exchanged a glance with James, who sat next to him, hands tight on the forward gun controls.

On the video screen in the aft compartment, Lydia saw what was happening on front view. The target ship was flying a panicked pattern of evasive dives and rolls now, but it couldn't shake them.

And the same trick of terrain wouldn't succeed twice.

Inexorably, the distance closed. Teri's vessel twitched and flailed like a frightened animal trying to get rid of an attacker whose teeth were locked on its tail. But all her efforts were futile.

James sighted the fire-control screen, locked on his

target, pressed the trigger. The jagged pattern of bolts homed in on the other vessel—closer, closer, closer—*hit!* There was a brief flare, then a blast that shattered the enemy vessel into shards spinning in all directions, dancing in fiery glow as they arced away from the center of the explosion, then cascaded down to the desert and woods below.

At the aft gun, Lydia frowned. She'd wanted to shoot the rogue down herself.

"That's it, Lydia," James said into his headset.

"No, it isn't," she snapped. "I still want Ham Tyler and the fifth-column traitor. Resume search pattern. Start from the area where we first spotted that intruder vessel. There's a good chance it was on its way to pick up Tyler. Now that we don't have to worry about anything in the air, divert all scanners to ground sweeps and cut our altitude. I want to see anything that moves down there."

"So much for help," Ham Tyler said.

He, Annie, and Barry could see the burning wreckage of Barry's aircraft farther down in the valley. They watched silently from the dubious haven of sparse woods.

"We can't stay here," Tyler concluded.

"Why not?" Annie said.

He pointed to the sky. Her eyes squinted against the stark cloudless blue, but she saw it. The Visitor skyfighter that had survived the encounter was heading toward *them*.

"Wait, Ham," she said. "We can hide."

"They'll find us sooner or later. And we've still got that invasion plan we've gotta get to the others. That's what all this was for."

Annie snorted ironically. "Hard to believe some theoretical strategy caused all this."

"Theoretical now, but deadly if Lydia gets to put it into effect," Barry pointed out, his alien voice throbbing with intensity.

"But there's no way back to civilization that doesn't take us out in the open, is there?" Ham asked.

Annie shook her head. "Nope. Of course, we could wait till dark."

"Same problem, Halsey," Ham said. "Where to hide so they can't find us." He shaded his eyes and searched the sky. "Oh, God."

Annie reacted sharply. "What?"

"Look—"

She and the Visitor followed Ham's pointing finger. The skyfighter was bearing down on their rest stop, moving slowly, as if stalking prey it knew was there.

"Halsey, get us out of here," Ham said.

"Ham, we can't. There's no way—"

Her argument was cut off by the streak of a laser blast from the sky. They were being shot at! The first line of tracer bolts sizzled the trees ten yards from their position, close enough to convince Ham the Visitors weren't simply guessing. They were trying to smoke their quarry out—but for capture or murder? He had no idea which, and didn't really care to stick around and find out.

"Now, Halsey!"

"There's a cave. If we can get to it without them actually seeing us, we might be able to fool 'em."

"Go!" Tyler barked.

Annie cut off the main trail into thicker foliage, and Ham and Barry followed. The stocky Visitor had trouble fitting through small openings in the bushes. Thorny branches ripped the artificial skin on his face and hands, revealing dark green, scaly hide.

Above them, the skyfighter had stopped shooting. It weaved unsteadily, like a hound sniffing for a lost scent.

They reached a clearing they'd have to cross, and Ham glanced over his shoulder. He saw the hesitation of the ship.

"This might be our only chance," he said. "Go!"

He pushed Annie ahead, then Barry, then plunged through the knee-high grass himself. In front of him, Barry stumbled and Annie stopped to help.

"No—keep moving!" Ham shouted, scooping the Visitor to his feet. They started running again. Ham sensed movement overhead, but before he could decide whether to look back, he felt the searing heat of a laser shot as it shrieked past his head. It barely missed them, blasting a hail of dirt clumps and sand into the air. He heard the incongruously faint hiss of the vessel's maneuvering thrusters as the pilot tried to hover steadily enough to allow the gunner a clean shot. A stream of laser bolts slashed the ground alongside as the trio kept running. Ham started a serpentine pattern, hoping to confuse the gunner by splitting their line into a multiple target. *They can't shoot all of us at once*, he thought as he swung his laser rifle up and fired at the ship.

The power of the energy streaks made the hair on Ham's neck prickle. Two incoming bolts sliced a heavy branch off a tree as the three of them ran past it. Annie tripped over the branch, her leg entangled in leafy twigs. Ham stopped this time.

"No! Get Barry and that plan to the cave—I'll catch up!"

Ham paused for a heartbeat, then turned and propelled Barry ahead of him. He fired at the skyfighter again, hoping the distraction would give Annie enough time.

She kicked at the branch and scrambled to her feet.

The skyfighter's cannon blazed again.

The laser bolts struck the ground inches from Annie—she leaped away, her eyes catching Ham's, urging him to *Go, don't wait*, and then the next barrage came. Ham had started to turn, to leave her behind, knowing she'd catch up, when he saw and heard—and *inhaled* the smell of burned flesh.

Annie was down, writhing in pain, smoke coming from an ugly scorch on her side. Ham skidded as he pushed Barry to cover in the trees just a few feet away. They were so close to shelter. . . .

In the time it took him to change direction, Annie became still. He reached her, ignoring the continuing fire from the ship overhead.

Sudden laser fire came from another source, and it was directed not at the ground, but at Lydia's ship. A glancing hit on the small aircraft's side rocked it and spun it halfway around.

"Ham, look!" Barry called.

Tyler ignored him, but Barry saw another Visitor vessel

streak across the sky. Lydia's damaged ship turned and limped toward this new attacker. Barry hurried out and helped Ham carry Annie to cover. They laid her gently on the dry yellow grass, where they saw that the burn went clear through her denim jacket, deep into her skin.

Tyler's hand waved helplessly over the wound, his face masked with grief. "Halsey, no . . . not now. We—we almost"—his voice choked down to a whisper—"almost made it."

Barry looked away, trying to locate the sounds of aerial combat. Then, in the distance he saw Lydia's ship circling like a wounded beast trying to keep its strong side to its enemy. But the attacker was too quick, peppering its target with warning shots. It kept missing, apparently intentionally.

Smoke filled the cabin of Lydia's skyfighter. One trooper lay dead on the deck, and the pilot worked valiantly to keep Lydia's tail gun facing the flitting enemy vessel which was shooting at will.

"Why don't they destroy us?" Lydia said almost to herself.

"They're toying with us," James answered from the front. "Lydia, we're running low on fuel. If we don't surrender, we'll crash."

Lydia heard him, but continued to angle her cannon in the futile search for a killing blow.

"Lydia!" James repeated. "We've got to land *now*!"

Her face screwed up in fury. "All right—land!" she spat.

"That's it!" Elias crowed from the cockpit of Zachary's borrowed ship. "They're goin' down!"

Maggie smiled from the pilot's seat next to him. Julie turned with a thumbs-up from the weapon turret in the rear. Zachary and the other resistance fighters in the midship cabin readied their weapons.

"Zachary," Julie called, "we need you now. Do your official act."

The Visitor climbed forward to the communications console next to Elias. He waited for Julie's signal.

"Maggie," Julie said, "follow them down, close but not too close, until we see how they react and until we know if Lydia's on that ship. Okay, Zach, your turn."

Elias activated the radio and Zach leaned in. "Disabled vessel, come in, please. I am speaking for Diana, the supreme commander. She knows about your unauthorized and bungled attempt to capture Donovan and Tyler, the human criminals. She has ordered you to cease your activities immediately and will be coming down to take command herself. You are also ordered to activate your locator beacon so she can find you upon her arrival," the young Visitor said with complete seriousness. "You will acknowledge this communication."

They all waited to see if a reply would come. Finally, Lydia's voice said: *"Orders acknowledged. Beacon activated."*

The signal from the downed ship locked on to the sensor screen while the ship's computer calculated the coordinates. Maggie changed her course accordingly and flew around a mountain. There, down in a dusty field, the disabled fighter squatted, vapor venting from its damaged engines, cabin door open, and Visitor soldiers climbing out.

"Okay, people, when we land, we mean business," Julie said. "If they even look like they're going to shoot, we shoot first. These uniforms should buy us a couple of seconds of surprise. Maggie, land head-on. I'll take the front laser to cover the rest of you. Elias, you're in charge of the landing detail."

"You got it, lady."

Maggie set their vessel down about ten yards away from Lydia's ship. The Visitors had been milling around, examining the scars of the brief dogfight, and the security commander had just ordered them into formation.

Elias peeked out the side port. "Line up them bowling pins, just line 'em up," he said. He looked back at the rest of the landing party standing with him at the two side hatches. Julie sat up front, next to Maggie, who remained at the pilot's controls. With both hands on the laser triggers, Julie nodded and Elias popped the hatches. He and the others jumped out, weapons raised.

Behind her dark glasses, Lydia's eyes narrowed. The troops from the other ship—*no helmets, no eye-protectors*.

"They're impostors," she growled. Then, loudly: "Weapons—open fire!"

The first reply came from Julie at the laser cannon, laying down a spray of energy bolts no more than a yard away from the Visitors' boots.

At the same time, Maggie spoke from the loudspeaker of the skyfighter: *"Don't move—hands in the air—or you'll be killed where you stand."*

Lydia did a double take as her shock troopers followed Maggie's instructions, totally oblivious to their commander's previous order. As if reading Lydia's mind, James turned to her and said, "I think your order's been countermanded."

For emphasis, Julie fired another short laser burst over the Visitors' heads. They ducked involuntarily, but kept their hands up. The rebels quickly relieved them of all weapons and hardware.

Inside the ship, Julie slid out of the weaponry seat. "Maggie, take the laser, just in case. Don't hesitate to fire if they rush us." She picked up a hand laser, then jumped down to the ground and walked over to the Visitor commander.

"Julie Parrish, isn't it?" Lydia said smoothly.

"Doesn't really matter, does it?" Julie asked rhetorically. "All that matters is that you didn't get what you came for."

"Hey, Julie—look," Elias called.

Julie turned to see Ham Tyler and Barry coming down from the nearby hills. She waited until Tyler reached them, and she was stunned by the hollowness in Tyler's usually unreadable eyes.

"Ham, what is it?" she asked, deeply concerned.

His lips twitched for just a second, and his eyes became masked again. "Nothing," he said in a monotone. He gave

Barry a quick glance, a tacit request for silence. The Visitor complied. Tyler handed the alien tape cassette to Julie. "This is Lydia's invasion plan. It's a doozy."

Julie took it. "We have it already," she said.

Ham's eyes flared, his jaw setting stiffly. "You *what*?"

"We have it already." She gestured at Zachary. "This is a real Visitor, and he brought us a second copy when Barry didn't come back or communicate with him. We were worried. We didn't know what might've happened to you all. Where're Mike and Chris?"

Ham shrugged. "I don't know. They were back in town. We don't even know if they're alive. But we do know Maragato was a phony, a Visitor passed off as the real thing."

"Jesus," Julie said.

"Got a lot of stories to tell each other, I'd guess," Ham said, glaring at Lydia, who was smiling now.

"I've got a—how do you humans say it?—punch line for this whole incident. This invasion plan of mine, which you now have two copies of? It was a fake—just as fake as Maragato."

Ham's teeth gritted and he stepped up to her. *"What?"*

Julie grabbed his shoulder. "Ham, don't forget the venom on their tongues."

But he was beyond hearing the warning or anything but what Lydia had to say.

She laughed. "You foolish humans. It was a lure to get you and Donovan out where we could control your actions and capture you to make up for the loss of the human spies you freed from us." She stopped laughing when Ham gripped her throat and dug his nails into her plastic flesh, tearing it down to the dark scales underneath. Lydia snarled and her tongue snaked ominously from between her lips.

"Don't threaten me, Lydia," Ham whispered. "Even if you blinded me, I'd still break your goddamned lizard neck."

James started to move toward his commander. Elias stepped in with his laser-rifle barrel. "Butt out, man."

Lydia tried to maintain a condescending smile as Tyler tightened his grip, his eyes slits of pure anger.

"Ham, don't," Julie said. Then, sharply: "Ham, *don't!* I don't know what happened out there, but this isn't the way to get her back!"

He let out a deep breath, his hand still clamped on Lydia's oozing neck, the oil from her natural skin shining in the sunlight. "Maybe for you people it isn't. This wouldn't be the first time I killed somebody with my bare hands," Tyler said calmly. "It was good enough for the other guys. It'd be good enough for this—*thing*," he said contemptuously.

"Well, if you're going to strangle her, hurry up," Julie said, impatience charging her voice.

Ham looked at her, surprise lifting his eyebrows. "You don't care?"

"No, I don't care. What I care about is getting to that town and getting Chris and Mike out—if they're still alive."

Suddenly Ham released Lydia, wiping his hand on her uniform. "Quick strangulation would be too good for her anyway. And, like you said, we don't have time now to torture her the right way."

"We're your prisoners then?" the Visitor security commander said.

Julie shook her head. "We don't take prisoners. You already know that. This is twice in one week you're getting away. I almost wish things had been different. I almost wished *you'd* attacked *our* ship. Then we would've had all the reason we'd need to blast you out of the sky. Maybe next time."

"That's not enough," Tyler said. "We need more Visitor uniforms. Get out of them."

Lydia straightened defiantly. "No."

Tyler nodded. "Yeah, Lydia, strip—you and your whole lizard pack here. The next time you see Diana, not only are you not gonna have your weapons or your ship, you're going to be buck naked."

He said it without a trace of humor, and Julie and the others wondered what could be fueling Ham Tyler's furnace of hate toward the invading aliens.

"A little light to undress by," Tyler added, walking over to the pile of newly liberated Visitor weapons and selecting a rifle. He set himself and fired a stream of energy bolts into the downed skyfighter, patiently holding the trigger until he hit something volatile and the ship exploded. Then he turned and came back to Lydia. He aimed the weapon at her midsection. "Do it—now. Or I'll burn you down before you can blink."

With a fractional nod to her troopers, Lydia undid the front of her uniform. The others followed her lead. Soon the red coveralls were in a neat pile, helmets and boots in rows—and Lydia and her ten surviving soldiers stood in the sun without a stitch of clothing on. Except for the gash in Lydia's neck, their human bodies were perfect specimens— firm and supple like retouched magazine photos. Utterly inhuman.

The Visitor gear was stowed in the skyfighter, and Julie ordered the resistance fighters in too. Maggie engaged the engines and the craft lifted off in a cloud of dust.

Ham sat in the rear gunner's nest alone, staring out the back port. No one tried to talk to him.

They landed in the center of Crow's Fork amid the burned-out hulks of two Visitor fighters and a land rover. There were no people to be seen anywhere. As she surveyed the ruins of alien vehicles and the smoking shell of O'Toole's house, Julie let out a low whistle.

"Good God, what happened here?"

Ham Tyler was next to her as they walked away from their aircraft. "If we can find Donovan and Chris, we'll find out."

"Where *is* everyone?"

"Maybe they're all dead. Lydia could've executed a whole town without losing too much sleep," Ham said.

Julie swallowed, hoping that wasn't true. "Maybe they just got scared when they saw us landing. For all they knew, Lydia was coming back. Damn—we've got to find *some- body* to talk to. Hey, let's try that general store."

Leaving Elias in charge of the ship, they crossed the street to the two-story wooden structure. As they ap- proached, they heard a creaking sound from the deep shadows of the front porch. Julie and Ham froze, weapons aimed.

"*You're* the ones in Visitor uniforms," called a familiar voice, "and *you've* got the nerve to draw on *us*?"

"Donovan!" Julie shouted.

He stepped down to the street, Chris and Frank O'Toole emerging behind him. Julie broke into a run and she and Donovan collided in a bear hug.

"What took you so long?" Chris said.

"We came as fast as we could. We came to save you." Then she giggled. "Jeez, I sound like Luke Skywalker."

"We saved ourselves," Donovan said.

"Oh, okay then." Julie disengaged from the embrace. "So long, guys," she said casually.

"Not so fast," Donovan said, quickly putting his arm around her waist.

"Hey," said an angry voice from the general-store doorway, "you didn't exactly save yourselves. You had a little help, huh?" It was Bradley, followed by Hank and Jacqueline. Bradley strutted proudly onto the street, a laser rifle at his side.

"Who are they?" Julie asked.

"Local militia," Donovan said. "Hey, Ham, where's Annie?"

Tyler's face reflected little, only grim tension. He met Donovan's probing gaze. "She's dead."

Donovan reacted, his eyes closing for a moment. "Damn," he said softly.

Julie seemed confused. "Who's Annie?" she asked, looking first to Tyler. Realizing she'd get no answer there, she searched Donovan's expression for a clue.

Donovan in turn looked to Ham for some sort of signal. *What should I say?* The lack of response from Tyler was signal enough.

"Who was she?" Julie repeated, very gently now.

"A friend," Donovan said. He locked his eyes on to Tyler's, trying to fathom this mysterious man who'd been both enemy and friend. *Ham, let us in,* Donovan thought. Then, for just a second, he caught a flicker of the private pain that Ham didn't dare share. The moment was fleeting, then gone, and Donovan wondered if it had been there at all.

Gray, impassive, the mask of Ham's face looked back at him. Donovan turned away first, toward Julie. "Let's get out of here," he announced.

"There's something I have to do first," Tyler said. "I, uh, I had to leave Annie out there in the woods. I want to bring her back."

"I'll help," O'Toole said.

But Ham shook his head. "I'd rather go by myself. Will you take care of everything after I leave her here?"

O'Toole nodded. "Of course, Tyler."

"I'll be back in a little while—it's not far." Tyler strode quickly to the skyfighter, climbed in, and lifted off.

The other resistance members and townspeople watched the Visitor craft fly toward the foothills.

"Uh, we have some prisoners here in town," O'Toole said after another moment of uncomfortable silence. "You're going to take them, aren't you?"

Julie frowned. "We can't."

"What do you mean, you can't?"

"Not permanently anyway," Donovan cut in. "We're just an underground group. We don't have any provisions for holding prisoners. It's not like we've got prisoner-of-war camps."

"Not in Nathan Bates-land," Julie added. "We're officially outlawed in the L.A. area, and it's too dangerous to transport prisoners to any facilities that might exist in areas under human control. So we just have to take their uniforms and weapons and spring 'em."

"Don't worry," Donovan said. "We'll transport the ones you've got on ice far enough from here that they won't crawl back and give you any grief."

"Which reminds me," Julie said, "we got quite a haul from Lydia's troops. There are a bunch of naked Visitors wandering somewhere in the foothills."

Donovan stared at her. "Huh?"

"You heard me."

"Now, that's something I'd like to see."

She smacked him playfully across the cheek. "Pervert. We also have two new recruits—Barry and Zachary have had their covers blown and can't go back to their Mother Ship. On balance, I'd say we gained a lot."

"Which reminds *me*," Donovan said suddenly, "what happened with the weapons shipment your group was gonna pick up?"

Julie rolled her eyes. "Hell—you *had* to ask? Bates intercepted the ship."

"You mean *your* cover is blown too?"

She shook her head. "No—thanks to Elizabeth. I don't know how that kid does it, but she sensed I'd be in grave danger if I boarded the ship, so I sent Kyle and Elias—and Bates was there to meet them."

"Damn him!" Donovan spat. "Did everybody get away okay?"

"Yeah. I can't figure Bates out, I really can't. He could have held them or used them to get to us, but he just let them go."

"The man's a real humanitarian," Donovan said sourly.

"Anybody need a cool drink?" Chris asked, turning toward the general store.

Donovan and Julie looked at each other. "Sure," they said in unison, then followed Chris inside.

It wasn't long before Tyler returned to town with Annie Halsey's body wrapped protectively in a blanket. O'Toole helped him carry her to the clinic, while Julie and Donovan gathered the rest of their rescue team at the skyfighter. They waited while Ham and the big Irishman conferred privately.

"Did she have any family?" Ham asked.

"No," O'Toole said. "There's a little stone church, an old Spanish structure, outside of town. She liked to go there."

Tyler managed an ironic smile. "I didn't know she was religious."

"Oh, she wasn't. She made a point *not* to go on Sundays. She'd go when there was no one else there. She believed in direct chats with the Almighty."

"That I can believe. Annie is—was—a very direct lady."

"And she liked to sit in the churchyard and look at the old gravestones, kind of commune with the spirits. I'll bury her there."

Tyler nodded. "That's good. I think she'd like that."

O'Toole gestured at the skyfighter, and he and Tyler walked toward it.

Julie and Donovan stood near the alien aircraft after everyone else had clambered aboard.

"You said we gained a lot," Donovan said, watching Ham and O'Toole. "Some of us also lost." Then he noticed Julie's face cocked to one side like a quizzical spaniel. He smiled at her, sadness in his eyes.

"Maybe one of these days I'll know what went on up here," she said.

"Don't count on it," Donovan replied.

With his teen militia in tow, O'Toole escorted Tyler to the skyfighter, then shook hands with Donovan and Julie.

"If you ever need us again . . ." O'Toole said.

"We'll try not to," Donovan said.

"Good-bye, Mr. O'Toole," Julie said, waving. "Good luck."

"Same to you—all of you."

Julie disappeared inside the overcrowded ship while O'Toole and the kids backed away. Tyler stood with one foot poised on the hatch sill. Donovan reached down to extend a hand. "You sure you don't want to stay?"

"Nope. Nothing to stay for."

Donovan moved out of the hatchway as Ham came up. "You okay, Ham?"

"This is a war, Gooder. People die. No big deal." Then he ducked inside.

Donovan took one last look at the dusty town, wishing Ham could get past that peculiar code of honor he lived by. Maybe he would the next time something like this happened. *I hope there never is a next time*, Donovan thought.

He shut the hatch and nodded to Maggie, who throttled the engines to maximum power. The skyfighter left Crow's Fork behind, lumbering as it gained altitude, and banked gently toward the south . . . toward home.

Written by . . .

. . . Howard Weinstein, who is also the author of *The Covenant of the Crown* (a *Star Trek* novel) and *V: East Coast Crisis* (with A. C. Crispin). Both these books reached bestseller lists immediately after publication. Howard's first professional writing was done for television: the *Pirates of Orion* episode of NBC's Emmy-winning animated *Star Trek* series in 1974, when he was a nineteen-year-old college junior. His other credits include columns and reviews in *The New York Times, Newsday,* and *Starlog* magazine, and he has won awards for writing and producing radio public-service announcements in New York.

Born in 1954, Howard Weinstein is a member of the biblical tribe called the Suburbanites, living near New York City with Mail Order Annie, his short but faithful Welsh Corgi (that's a dog). Annie doesn't read much, but she once tried to eat a book by a rival author.

Over the years, Howard has become a familiar guest speaker at East Coast science fiction and *Star Trek* conventions.

Watch for

THE ALIEN SWORDMASTER

the next V book from Pinnacle

coming in April!

61

YOU WATCHED IT ON TV...

NOW
DISCOVER
THE STARTLING
TRUTH
BEHIND
THE
INVASION...

...as the ultimate battle for survival continues...